PRAISE FOR *BUDDY—I*

"Holly Schlaack has written a unique book that gives readers a view of the perspective of a small child in the foster care system. As a former county prosecuting attorney, I have had first-hand experience with kids in the foster care system. And, as Ohio Attorney General, I have seen the need for foster families dramatically increase as the opiate crisis has continued to plague our state. I hope readers will pick up this book, learn more about what foster kids face in their daily lives, and be moved to help kids like Buddy."

—*Mike DeWine, Ohio Attorney General*

"*Buddy* is a masterful, once-in-a-decade real-world intersect of child and community. Too many times, the accounts of abused or neglected children go untold; rarely are their stories heard from a child's perspective. The author blends this intersection by illustrating–through the eyes of a baby–daily life in the foster care system."

—*Jon Fishpaw, System Vice President of Advocacy and Government Relations, Mercy Health*

"I did not expect to so thoroughly enjoy reading about kids in the foster care system – or to have such a deep and visceral reaction seeing life through the eyes of little Buddy. This is required reading for anyone who cares about kids and the future of our society."

—*Laren Bright, Award-Winning Children's Television Animation Writer*

"Telling the story of the successes and failures of the foster system through little Buddy's eyes is a stroke of genius. It wasn't until I became a foster mom that I realized the overwhelming number of invisible foster children in my own community, and the desperately under-resourced network of foster families and case workers who do so much with so little. A must-read for anyone considering becoming a foster parent or adopting through the foster system."

—*Alissa Hauser, The Pollination Project Foundation*

"The crisis of babies in foster care impacts every one of us, because untreated, their problems grow up right alongside the children and become vastly more costly and harder to heal as they grow older. We should care, not just because they are innocent human beings, but because done badly, our government interventions create successive generations of expensive, broken grown-ups: over $50 billion a year in direct and consequential cost, a great deal of it avoidable... but we are not good at that.

This innovative book brings the hidden world of foster babies into the spotlight through the eyes of Buddy, a foster baby who teaches us how simple his needs are, and how easily they are overlooked by the very child welfare system created to protect him. The story of Buddy comes at a time when foster care is overflowing with 437,000 infants, children, and youth in desperate need of safety, stability, and love. Hope only wins when we say yes to getting involved in the lives of these most vulnerable and defenseless citizens. Your first step is reading this book."

—*Peter Samuelson, President and CEO, First Star, Inc., www.firststar.org*

BUDDY
View From The Pumpkin Seat

ALSO BY HOLLY SCHLAACK

Invisible Kids–Marcus Fiesel's Legacy

One short life, one terrible death and 12 things
YOU can do to improve the lives of foster children.

BUDDY

VIEW FROM THE PUMPKIN SEAT

HOLLY SCHLAACK

Author of the acclaimed *Invisible Kids*

ADVOCACY
PUBLISHING

Cincinnati, Ohio

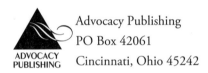 Advocacy Publishing
PO Box 42061
ADVOCACY
PUBLISHING   Cincinnati, Ohio 45242

First Edition

ISBN 978-0-9996562-0-4 print
ISBN 978-0-9996562-1-1 e-book
Library of Congress Control Number: 2017963576

This is the story of Buddy, a nine-month-old baby, who enters the foster care system following neglect and endangerment at the hands of his mother. Written in the first-person perspective, Buddy chronicles his journey through several homes during which time he forms important ideas about himself, others and the world around him.

Drawing from the author's extensive experience working in the foster care system and the science of child development, this book offers a rare glimpse into the heart and mind of a very vulnerable infant who is deeply impacted by his experiences.

Book Designer: Patricia Bacall
Copywriter: Laren Bright
Cover Illustration: Shielaugh V. Divelbiss
Editor: Proofed to Perfection

Printed in the United States of America on acid-free paper.

www.booksbyholly.com

DEDICATION

For Buddy–and all foster babies. May you know and find Love.
For Tori Sandoval–your short life and brutal death will not be in vain.
We promise.

ACKNOWLEDGMENTS

IT'S BEEN SAID IT TAKES a village to raise a child. I think it takes a village to move a book from idea to completion. This story is the result of many people who helped bring *Buddy* to life.

A very talented team came together to give this story the polish, shine and package it deserves. I'm deeply grateful for the efforts of Patricia Bacall, Laren Bright, Shielaugh Divelbiss and our friends at Proofed to Perfection. Their collaborative spirit and commitment to this project have been spectacular.

My sister, Gretchen Eck, became a foster parent and in the process, I became a foster aunt. This gave me an entirely different perspective I'd never had as a former children's services caseworker and former Guardian ad Litem (GAL). Getting to love, babysit and occasionally provide overnight care for each of her foster babies deepened my resolve to give these infants a voice.

My former colleague, Kate Merrilees, introduced me to the world of babies and taught me nearly everything I know about understanding and helping those who were abused and neglected. I'm a better person, mother and child advocate because of her.

Years ago, I was fortunate to have two people come into my life. Kelly Gries, a fellow child advocate, mother of twelve and champion of all children has been a ray of light and hope throughout my evolving career. Mayo Woody, a former foster and adoptive parent, showed me how greatly we all benefit when we keep dialoging and working together despite our differences. In 2014, Kelly, Mayo and I combined our passion and gifts to launch Invisible Kids Project, a non-profit dedicated to prioritizing the rights of kids in the child welfare system and engaging community in creating positive systemic change. I'm thankful for them and many others including Jenny Adamson, Bob and Chris Santoro, and Barb Wehmann and Ed Lentz for working with us to realize our vision of a transformed child welfare system.

Finally, I'm indebted to Sue Gall and Julie Murray, whose wisdom and guidance have a deep and lasting impact.

My former teacher, friend and spiritual mentor, Father Larry Tensi, started encouraging me to write when I was sixteen. He hasn't stopped. Every time I got 'stuck' writing this book, he moved me forward with suggestions. When I nearly abandoned it altogether, he reminded me of its purpose and insisted I keep going. When I complained about needing a good place to write, he offered up space at his parish, St. Columban in Loveland, Ohio. His friendship and steady presence in my life are anchors I've come to rely on. They have made all the difference.

Writing is a solitary endeavor which isn't always easy for an extrovert like me. Luckily, my wickedly funny and endlessly talented friend, Chris Santoro, makes it much more enjoyable. Her input makes my writing better and her friendship makes my life brighter. My sister, Barb Rengering, also makes my life brighter in countless ways. She is my biggest cheerleader and motivates me to be the best person I can be. Her support and encouragement are tremendous gifts.

Most of all, my gratitude goes to my husband, Ed. Together we built a perfectly imperfect life rooted in love. Our three kids, Hanna, Grace and Ben are our greatest gifts. They inspire and challenge us, make us proud and make us laugh. What a joy to watch their lives unfold. We love each of them more than they could ever know.

A FEW WORDS FROM THE AUTHOR...

I WAS A TWENTY-TWO-YEAR-OLD COLLEGE GRADUATE, and only three weeks post graduation, when I started my first "real" job as a children's services caseworker. Most of the time, I was overwhelmed with little supervision or mentoring to help guide me through the daily life-and-death decisions I made. Case by case, kid by kid, I did the best I could and prayed it was enough. Looking back, I am stunned by the great responsibility placed on such young and inexperienced shoulders.

Fast-forward more than two decades later. I was making an unexpected stop at the store to buy a winter hat for the cranky infant sitting in the pumpkin seat I carried. He was my sister's foster baby, and my responsibility while she was away overnight. The little guy had just returned, minus his hat and one sock, from a supervised visit with his biological parents. He was out of sorts and unhappy. Missing his nap didn't help either.

Two women behind the counter began to ring up my purchases while I talked quietly to him and rocked him in his seat.

"It must be so hard to be a baby," one said jokingly. Being this baby is definitely hard, I thought. His whole life is up in the air, and he's constantly at the mercy of whatever the court and caseworkers decide.

"No kidding," the other one replied. "Not a care in the world. Someone to take care of your every need." I just smiled, hiding my slight annoyance. If only they knew what I knew.

"Yep, all he has to do is eat and sleep. Nothing more," the first one laughed.

"Except wear cute clothes," the second one said as she held up a sweater I couldn't resist buying. "Can't forget the cute clothes!" This time they both laughed. On a better day, I might have too.

"Poor thing. What a rough life." The friendly banter continued as my smile faded, my patience worn thin for no good reason. They couldn't be faulted for their assumptions.

"I wish my life was that easy." By then, I couldn't bear to keep my mouth shut. Who was I protecting by staying quiet anyway?

"Actually," I began, trying to sound helpful, "life really isn't easy at all when you're born premature and drug dependent, bounced around in foster care, and just coming from a visit with your biological parents."

They were still picking their jaws up off the floor after I paid and left.

"I know it's hard," I told my little guy as I kissed him on the forehead. "I wish they knew too." For a split second, he stopped fussing and we locked eyes. In that sliver of time, the idea for this book was born.

Buddy is a fictional story based on snippets of dozens and dozens of real stories. Nearly everything you are about to read is something I've directly witnessed or heard said as a former children's services caseworker, a former Guardian Ad Litem (GAL) and CASA Program Manager, and a foster aunt. Sadly, there's no need for much embellishment when it comes to child welfare.

This book also draws on the latest information about how infants experience the world. Thanks to emerging research, we know babies are far more sophisticated than we ever realized. In their earliest days, they empathically cry if they hear other infants cry. At age five months, they can read emotion in adults. By nine months, they appear to understand the concept of friendship.

Most importantly, we are learning about the power of loving relationships to mitigate trauma and help babies grow and thrive. An ongoing connection to a nurturing adult who responds and protects is more than a basic need. It is a right—one the child welfare system too often ignores, despite science and common sense.

Denying babies, or any children, access to such relationships sets them up for a lifetime of suffering and increases the likelihood of mental health and addiction challenges, educational and behavioral difficulties, and chronic health conditions throughout their lives.

Elevating a child's right to such relationships above all else dramatically increases his or her chance for a happy, healthy childhood and future. It means a better future for all of us.

People often ask me how I can stay in this field for so long when it is so depressing. My answer is always the same: I stay because

I know that as a society, together we can create a better system that protects and nurtures more children and families to their full potential. I stay because I've seen miracles and lives transformed. I stay because the pain of staying is nothing compared to the joy of knowing my work has changed the course of a child's life...and the lives of the next generation.

I stay for Love.

I invite you to step into Buddy's world and see the power of Love unfold. It is always, always there. You just have to look for it.

—Holly Schlaack, January 2018

CHAPTER 1

I DON'T FEEL SO GOOD. I usually never do, but this is worse. And scary.

The straps on my car seat are cutting into my shoulders. I'm used to stuff hurting, but not like this.

I'm moving so fast my belly tumbles up and down. If I had bigger hands, I'd hold onto the sides for dear life, but I can't. I'm too little.

The man driving is screaming at my mom and she is screaming at him, too. They do that a lot. I never scream, though. I did a few times and that was a *really* bad idea. It made everything way worse. That's when I learned a new trick. It's my disappearing trick. I stay very quiet and pretend no one can see or hear me.

We go faster and faster and the screaming gets louder. It's always a little crazy with these people, but not *this* crazy.

I shut my eyes as tight as I can to make the flashing lights go away. My ears hurt from the pounding sirens. *Screeeeech.* I slam against the straps in my car seat so hard maybe my head will pop off. I can't breathe.

The car doors swing open and my mom and the man run fast, fast, far away from me. Cold air hits my face. It feels good, so I take a deep breath even though the air makes my eyes water and my throat itchy. I have no idea what to do, not that there's much I can do anyway.

So I just sit and wait for what will come next. I've been around long enough to know Something *always* comes next. Sometimes it's better. Usually it is worse. It's always a little scary, no matter what.

A bright light slowly moves across the car, so I try my disappearing trick. I stay as still as I can and don't even move a finger. The light creeps closer and closer until it shines on the edge of my seat and hits my face. My heart is pounding. My disappearing trick won't work.

The Something Next is here.

"Well, well, little buddy, what do we have here?"

The light makes a circle above my head and two big, warm hands loosen the tight straps. I come face to face with a big man I've never seen before. He wears a hat on his giant head and he's dressed in a dark color. I don't know who he is or what he will do to me.

All I know is, I can't just stay quiet and out of the way. I can't go anywhere or do anything. I'm just *here* and scared and tired and hungry. There's only one thing left to do at a time like this. I close my eyes and scream and scream and scream as loud and hard as I can.

I might never stop.

The thing about screaming is, it does stop. It has to. And since my superpower is not screaming forever, I'm going to have to stop eventually.

Might as well be now.

My screaming settles into crying and I open my eyes.

"Hush now, little buddy, you're okay." Warm Hands is talking softly. His arms are wrapped around me and I lay against his chest while he slightly sways. His huge hands are kind of scratchy. Who cares?

I look for my mom but I don't see her anywhere. I don't see the man who lives with us either.

I think they left me. I hope Warm Hands doesn't leave me, too.

I might be just a baby, but I know all about hands. I've felt all kinds of hands since I got here ten months ago and trust me, some are good and some are bad. Some hands, like the ones driving the car, are rough. Sometimes I'm sleeping and those hands just pick me up by my leg. When I'm hungry, sometimes those hands shove a bottle into my mouth so hard, I can't breathe.

But some hands are good though, like Warm Hands, which took me out of that smoky car where my mom left me. Or the hands of the two ladies who live next door with a bunch of kids. Their hands always make me feel better.

My mom's hands are the hardest to figure out. Sometimes they do things like hold me and feed me and then suddenly *bam*, they turn mean and they hurt. One time, her hand pinched me under my arm. Another time, it hit me hard on my leg. With her, I never know for sure which hands I'm going to get, but at least I'm used to it. Besides, usually they're better than they are bad.

"It's freezing," Warm Hands says to a lady wearing a hat just like Warm Hands. She wraps a soft blanket around me and I peek out from its edge. There are lots of cars with red and blue lights, but they aren't loud anymore. I'm glad.

"Poor thing," the lady says. "He's filthy. Probably has bed bugs. Don't take 'em home with you."

"I know. I hope he doesn't. If he does, well, I guess that's just another job hazard." Warm Hands pauses before he talks again. "Did you see the back seat? I can't for the life of me understand how a parent can deal drugs with a baby in the back seat—not to mention taking him on a high-speed chase and then abandoning him."

"They're the kind who probably shouldn't have a kid in the first place," she tells him. "It's happening more and more. Last week, it was a toddler. The week before that, ages four and five."

"I just can't wrap my head around it, no matter how many times I see it. I mean, aren't parents supposed to have some kind of instinct to protect that kicks in?"

"Not if addiction trumps it." The woman reaches out and rear-ranges the blanket so it covers all of me, including my head. "I never get used to seeing it either, though. I wish we had a hat for him. Not much hair to cover that little head. He's gotta be cold."

Being a little cold is the least of my problems. Besides, it's better than being stuck in that smoky car.

"Somehow, I'm not surprised his parents didn't think to grab a hat for him," Warm Hands replies. He's still swaying, just a tiny bit. It feels good here in his arms.

"Any idea what his name is?"

"Nope, but he sure can scream. Right, Buddy?" I think about

looking up at Warm Hands' face, but I'm too scared, so I don't.

"Maybe he's hungry. Does he have a bottle?" she asks.

"Not one fit for a baby to touch, let alone drink out of. It was laying on the seat next to him, along with some dirty needles. There was a diaper bag in the back of the car. Not much in it, just a couple diapers. Some kind of dirty outfit. I hoped we'd find something with his name, but there's nothing."

"You need this?" A man walks toward us carrying my seat.

"His pumpkin seat? How's the condition?" Warm Hands asks.

"Surprisingly, it's a new model and looks alright. Should be safe to keep as a car seat. Just a little dirty. Reeks of cigarette smoke."

"I'll take it," the lady says and the man hands it over.

"Dan, we need you over here," a deep voice calls out. There are different voices everywhere. I'm used to lots of voices, so they don't bother me.

"Can you take him?" Warm Hands asks the woman. She sets my seat on the ground and holds out her arms. I move from him to her. The blanket slips off my head.

"Please don't have bed bugs," she says very quietly, like she doesn't want anyone to hear her. Her hands are soft, not scratchy. I liked his better, though.

"It's gonna be okay, Buddy." Warm Hands says as he pulls the blanket up so it rests on my head again. He pauses, and I think about looking for his face, but I don't.

"Dan, you coming?" There's that deep voice again. Warm Hands doesn't move. I think he wants to stay here.

"Dan, go. We have an ambulance a couple minutes out. They'll take care of Buddy. Don't worry."

"You're in good hands, little buddy. You're safe now." I like his voice. He leans in and puts his hand on my belly but I still don't look at his face. Then he's gone.

There are more people in dark colors, but I don't know where they all came from. A big box on wheels with more flashing red lights comes and another lady hops out and walks toward us.

"Let's get him to the hospital," she says as she looks down at my car seat on the ground. "Is this his?"

"Yeah."

"Let's get him in it and load him up." She reaches down and lifts my seat by the handle.

Once I'm back in my seat, she puts me into the big box on wheels and then climbs in beside me. It's very bright in here. It hurts my eyes. It smells strange, too. I don't like it. The whole thing starts to move and those sirens are pounding in my ears again. My lip is quivering. I try not to, but I start to cry. I wish I knew some of these hands. I wish I could have the hands of one of the ladies who live next door.

The doors of the big box swing open and a fresh blast of cold air hits my face. I have no idea where I'm going, but I don't like it. It is bright and loud and everything is moving so fast my head hurts.

This would be a good time to use my disappearing trick, but it won't work. All my insides are buzzing around and even though I want to close them, my eyes are stuck open.

"Baby boy found in the back seat of a car abandoned following a high-speed chase. Car is registered to an Erica Wilson. Two suspects, one male, one female, fled the scene on foot. This is all we have," one lady says to another as she holds up my diaper bag. There are so many different voices and faces. They all swirl together.

My eyes are still stuck open, and suddenly there's another new face right in front of mine. My heart pounds. I can't go anywhere, so I just turn my head to the side so I don't have to see it anymore.

"Hey there, little guy. You've had a big night. A scary night, for sure. Don't you worry, though, we've got you." This nice voice soothes my insides a little bit, but I still don't look to see where it's coming from.

"Do we have a name or date of birth?" the nice voice continues.

"Not yet. They're working on it."

"Well, I bet you wish you could tell us what it is. Don't worry. We'll find it soon enough." I like this nice voice. I'm pretty sure it is talking to me. I love when people talk to me. It's my favorite thing, but it hardly ever happens.

"Apparently, while he was with the police, he picked up a nickname. Buddy."

"Buddy's a good name," Nice Voice says. "What do you think?"

I slowly turn my head so I can see a little of her face, but not all of it, and definitely not the eyes. I never look in eyes because they scare me. My lip starts to quiver and I spiral into my second screaming fit of the day.

"Um, I don't think he likes it, Maggie."

"Sure he does. He's just tired of sitting in his pumpkin seat." She reaches in to unbuckle the straps. "Here, let's get you out of that thing."

I stop crying soon after I'm in Maggie's arms. She has good hands. I can just tell.

"See? I told you. He just wanted out of that seat, didn't you, Buddy?"

I like that she talks to me. I look at a little bit more of her face and I don't feel scared.

After forever, I've been poked and prodded and bathed and fed. So many faces come and go, but Maggie stays with me and holds me the whole time. She talks to me a lot, too. I love that!

My scared has gone away now and I'm actually feeling pretty good. My belly is full and my bottom feels amazing. I was used to it stinging all the time, but Maggie cleaned me all up and put this stuff on it to make the sting go away. Not a single hand has hurt me—well, except for this one time when a man in a white coat pressed on my belly. He's just finished poking around when a new face comes to the door.

There have been so many new faces today! I can't keep up.

"Hello, I'm Todd. Children's Services." The new man holds out his hand to the man in the white coat.

"Nice to meet you, Todd. I'm Dr. Pearson and this is Maggie. She's been in charge of this little guy since they brought him in. She was coming off a double two hours ago, but she offered to stay until you arrived. He seems to like her more than anyone else who's been in here."

"I'm sorry I couldn't get here sooner. It's been a little bit crazy today."

"Do you have an identity for him? We've been calling him Buddy," says White Coat.

"Michael Wilson, nine months old. We tracked it down through his mom's name when the police called it in. We've had contact with this family before. Closed out three months ago, unsubstantiated abuse allegation. That's pretty much all we got," Todd says.

"I was hoping you could fill in some blanks. Do you have any birth or medical history? Family history? Shot records? Anything?" White Coat asks.

"Nothing like that." Todd shakes his head. "We got his identifying information from our system. His closed-case file still needs to be pulled from our records department, but I doubt it has anything related to birth or medical records. From how he looks right now, do you have any concerns?"

"A few. For one, he's got a terrible diaper rash, bordering on infection. He may have some reflux. He's spit up quite a bit, but that could just be all the commotion he's been through today. Or it could be the formula. There's no way to know for sure. He's pretty congested, too."

Todd is scribbling lots of notes on a pad of paper and nodding.

"It also looks like he has some significant developmental delays. By now, he should be crawling and pulling up on things, getting ready to walk. He's not nearly there," White Coat says.

"Significant?" Todd asks.

"Well, definitely concerning. Look at this. Maggie, will you stand up?" Maggie stands with me in her arms. "Do you see how his body just kind of dangles there?"

They all look at me while my arms and legs hang. They don't really do anything. I rest my head on Maggie's shoulder.

"Basically, he hasn't moved around enough to develop his muscles, so he doesn't really have any strength. He's probably been left in a crib or somewhere without much interaction."

"I can see that now," Todd says. "I don't have kids, so I'm not that familiar."

"Also, take a look at the back of his head. It's flat—an indication

7

that he's been left for long periods of time on his back. That's not good," White Coat explains. "He's going to need a full developmental assessment and services such as physical therapy, I'm sure. The sooner, the better."

"Of course. I'll put in a referral. I'm an intake worker, so I won't have the case for long, but I'll make sure the paperwork gets in this week. The ongoing worker will have to follow up on it. I'll get the ball rolling, though. Is there anything else?"

"He's right in the thirtieth percentile for height, but his weight is in the tenth. We'd like those numbers to be a little closer together. He's a little thing for his age, but it's hard to tell if there's a problem without knowing his birth weight and without access to his growth charts over the past ten months. If his parents are petite, chances are he will be, too. Speaking of his parents, any word on them?"

"No. The two suspects in the car are still on the run. I'm assuming he's going to be discharged? I mean, if you kept him, that would give us more time to find a foster home, but I know there's probably no reason for you to keep him." Todd looks at the phone in his hand.

"I don't see a need to admit him. I've prescribed an antibiotic cream for his diaper rash. It will need to be applied at every change, which should be at least every two hours. We'll send a sample with him. Should last a couple days, until the prescription gets filled. He needs to see a pediatrician within a week for a follow-up and a full exam. If the congestion gets any worse or he has any trouble breathing, bring him back immediately. I'd like to speak with his foster parents. Would that be possible?"

Todd shakes his head.

"We don't even have custody of him yet. My supervisor's working on the paperwork now. Then we'll start looking for a home."

"It's already past five-thirty. Isn't court closed?" White Coat looks confused.

"Yeah, but there's always a judge on call for these situations. We can't place a kid in foster care without a court order. The judge can grant custody over the phone. There'll be a hearing in the morning," Todd explains.

Maggie sits back down with me in her arms and I put my head on her chest again. With my ear against her, I can hear the slightest *thump thump*. Inside of me, I feel my own *thump thump* in my chest and it moves the same as hers. Her finger traces small circles on the top of my ear and the rhythm of it all soothes everything inside of me and out.

My eyes are getting heavy. I'm so comfy, I want to stay right here forever.

CHAPTER 2

MY HEAD ROLLS TO ONE side, and then the other, and when I open my eyes the lights are dim and I hear strange noises from far away, but I don't make any noise. I'm used to waking up and just lying there, so that's what I do for a while. Eventually, my belly starts rumbling again and the sting on my bottom is back. I make a tiny sound and Maggie appears. She scoops me up.

"Hey there, Buddy. Did you have a nice nap?" I just look at her. She keeps talking while she carries me across the room, lays me down, and begins to change my diaper. I let out a big yawn.

"I hear you," Maggie says in a happy voice. For the first time all day, I smile. "You're not the only one who's sleepy. I think I dozed off, too. I was tired when my shift ended. Feels like a week ago! I couldn't leave you, though, not until you were safely on your way. I sure do hope you go to a good home. Todd's working on it. He seems like a nice guy and a good worker. You are very lucky." She puts more of that white cream on my bottom. I'm in heaven.

The door opens. It's Todd. He's talking on the phone and writing on a piece of paper. That's a lot of things to do at one time. Maybe it's one of his tricks.

"What's the news?" Maggie asks as she finishes pulling up my pants. We are eye-to-eye and, for the first time ever, I don't look away. She smiles at me then touches the tip of my nose with her finger. I watch her every move and smile, too. She carries me across the room and starts to make a bottle.

"The judge awarded emergency custody. My office faxed the papers over here a while ago. We finally have a home that will take him. It only took three hours and sixteen phone calls before we finally got a 'yes'."

"Are the foster parents going to come and get him?" Maggie asks.

"Yeah, right. In our dreams. We're lucky we even found a home for him. Finding foster parents willing to come to come to the hospital … that's a tall order."

"It shouldn't be," Maggie says quietly.

Is she talking to me? I don't think so, because she's not making any fun sounds. But she's looking at me while I'm looking at her, filling my belly with this bottle and making me feel like all is right in my world.

"I couldn't agree more. But we have to take what we can get and sadly, we don't always have many options."

"It really would be nice if the foster parents came here. Not that it's any of my business, but I kind of want to meet the people who will be taking him. I mean, I'd take him home with me …"

"It's never that simple," Todd sighs. "He has to go to a certified foster home."

"I know," Maggie sighs. "I just wish he didn't have to. He's so sweet, and I think I'm growing on him. Look, I can make him smile." She picks me up and makes silly noises and I smile all the way across my face. "It took all day to get him to do that. It was the hardest work I've done today. And I'm a trauma nurse!" They are both laughing. I like that sound.

White Coat appears and he and Todd start talking. Who knows what they're saying? Not me, because I don't care. I'm just enjoying my bottle and snuggling in Maggie's arms. After a while, she lifts me to her shoulder and pats my back. I let out a big burp and smile again.

Todd and White Coat keep talking while Maggie holds me close. Eventually, Todd and White Coat leave the room together. I don't know where they go.

"Now you listen here, Buddy." Her voice is quiet. I look in Maggie's eyes and they don't scare me at all. I could stay with her forever.

"There's something really special about you. I can feel it. No matter what happens next, you will always be loved. Don't you forget it." She holds me tight and kisses me on my forehead.

White Coat and Todd return with my diaper bag and car seat. Maggie hands me over to Todd, but I don't want her to. I want to stay in her arms with her safe hands and I want to hear her happy voice talk to me the way no one has ever talked to me. Somehow, I know Maggie doesn't want to hand me over either, but I guess it doesn't matter because Todd is strapping me into my car seat. Suddenly, I'm scared again.

I know it's time again for Something Next. I just have no idea what it is.

It's dark outside when Todd knocks on the door. A lady opens it and Todd walks inside the narrow door frame and into a small room that is dark, too. Todd puts me and my seat down on the floor and sets my diaper bag on a couch.

"Mrs. Fremont, this here is Michael." Todd reaches down and unfastens the buckles. He pulls me up and puts me in another new set of arms. She holds me upright and looks me over from head to toe.

"Is this all he has?" she asks, eyeing the diaper bag.

"I'm afraid so," Todd says. He sounds sad and tired. "It's more than he had early this morning when the police found him in the back of a car. The hospital sent a couple of outfits—there's a spare in the bag—and enough diapers to get you through the night. Speaking of diapers, he's got a sample of antibiotic cream for a diaper rash here and a prescription that will need to be filled tomorrow. It's pretty bad. You'll need to change him at least every two hours to clear it up."

Todd hands her the prescription and pulls out a packet of information.

"Here's all the information we have on him. There's not much, though," Todd tells her as he hands over an envelope.

"What about formula? I don't have anything here. When your office called and asked if we'd take him, we said no at first. We've fostered for more than twenty years, but we're getting too old for this near middle-of-the-night business. But they said they called over a dozen other homes and nobody would take him. So here we are. Lordy, I hope I don't regret this!"

I don't know what to think about This Lady and I'm not sure

about her hands, either. I can't tell if they are hands that hurt or hands that don't. They don't feel bad … but they don't feel good, either.

"Thank you for saying yes," Todd says. "Honestly, if you hadn't, I don't know where he'd go, except back to the night staff at the office, and we try to avoid that if we can."

The lady just stares at him.

"Anyway, the hospital sent some formula and bottles, too. They're in his diaper bag. He had a bottle about an hour ago. He has some spitting up issues that you need to watch. Oh, and he's congested, and if he shows any signs that he's having trouble breathing, you need to call 911."

"Wait one minute. Nobody said anything about trouble breathing and 911," This Lady says. "We don't take medically fragile kids."

"He's not medically fragile. He's just a little congested. The problem is, we have no prior medical information about him, so we have to be extra careful until we know more. He may just have the sniffles," Todd explains. This Lady doesn't look happy. There's a long pause while This Lady thinks.

"Oh, alright," This Lady says with a big sigh. "How often does he eat? Is he on a schedule?"

"Your guess is as good as mine. When he's hungry, I suppose he'll let you know." Todd is looking at his phone again. "Look, I need to head out. It's been a long day and I'm due in court first thing in the morning." He leans toward me and stretches his hand out to pat me on the head. "See you soon, Buddy."

"Buddy?" This Lady says. "I thought you said his name was Michael."

"Oh yeah, it is Michael, but he picked up this nickname today before we knew his real one. I guess it just kind of stuck," Todd explains. "I'll be in touch." He walks out the door into the dark. This Lady looks at me. I look away.

"Michael, Buddy, whatever," she says as she sets me down on the couch and opens my diaper bag. "Goodness, this thing smells just like his pumpkin seat," she mutters. She pulls out a clear plastic bag with my one-piece bear outfit and sticks her nose in it. "Ugh, this is even worse. Throwing that one out!"

A man shuffles into the room and flips on a bright light. I shut my eyes as tight as I can.

"I can't believe they sent us another baby. I thought those days were over. And I sure thought they were over when I took down the crib. We don't even have it up. It's in the garage somewhere. Did you tell them that?" Man asks.

"Yes, I did, but they said this is an emergency placement and it's fine as long as we have it up tomorrow. He'll have to sleep in his pumpkin seat tonight." This Lady's voice doesn't make me feel good inside.

"Well, I guess I know what I'm doing tomorrow," Man says. He picks up the envelope that Todd gave to This Lady. "Is this his information?"

"Yes, but I haven't looked at it yet," she says.

"You're not missing much," Man says as he fumbles through the papers. "Let's see, so far we have a name, a birth date, and the name of his mom. There's a dad listed here, too. That's it. Nothing else." He puts the papers down on a table. "I'm going back to bed. You coming?" He's already turned around and started walking away.

"In a minute," she calls after him. She lays me down and checks my diaper. It is mostly dry, so she puts a little more white cream on my bottom. "This looks awful." She's shaking her head, but I don't know if she's talking to me. I'm just glad my bottom feels better.

She picks me up and puts me back in my seat. She fastens the straps, turns out the bright light, and follows Man down the hall.

I'm alone again.

I'm not sure what to do with this part of Something Next, so I don't do anything except sit in my seat. I actually don't mind. I've spent *a lot* of time in my seat for my whole life, and I'm used to it. Besides, the smell of my seat is the only thing I know, and what I know is always less scary than what I don't know. Everything now is different: this room, This Lady and Man, everything. I sit here in my seat for a long, long time until my eyes feel so heavy, I can't keep them open any longer.

CHAPTER 3

I FIDGET IN MY SEAT AND wiggle my bottom all around. Everything feels mushy down there and boy, does it hurt! I open one eye, then the other, and I don't remember seeing any of this before. Of course, there's not much to see from my seat on the floor. At least I have my seat, even if people think it stinks.

The room is dark but a little light comes in through the windows and shows up in lines across the wall. This kind of dark is my favorite. It's not too dark and scary with just all black, but it's not too bright, either. Sometimes the bright hurts my eyes and then my head starts to hurt, too.

There's not much to see, but there's a lot to hear. Voices and laughing mixed in with all other kinds of noise run together. I think I know those sounds. They come from a big box where colors change all the time. I look around and yes, there it is, high above me and off to one side. I've seen this thing before. There was one in the place where I lived with my mom. It was always there and always making noise. It's here, too.

I'm all hot and sweaty and my bottom is killing me. So is my belly. Usually, I wait as long as I can before I make any noise. It's a trick I learned when I lived with my mom. If I made too much noise too many times, then her hands would hurt. There were lots of different hands that came and went out of the place where I lived with my mom. They were always big and strong and rough.

The voices that came with those hands were always deep and mad. I tried to avoid those hands as much as I could, even if sometimes I couldn't help it because my belly would hurt so much, I had to do something.

I sit here in my seat until I can't stand it anymore. I'm going to have to make some noise. Whatever comes will come. I take a deep breath and start to cry.

Long legs are standing in front of my seat. I don't know where these long legs will end or what's on top of them. Long arms reach down and pick up my seat and I go up-up-up in the air and come face-to-face with Something Next.

It's Man. I remember him now. I saw him last night when I came to this place.

"Cynthia, the baby's awake," Man calls out as he lifts me out of my seat. So far, so good. His hands don't feel good or bad; they just hold me out and my body dangles. His face is in front of mine.

"Hurry up now, Mama. This baby *stinks*. And from the looks of his scrunched-up face, he's headin' for a screaming fit that just might never stop."

"I'm coming. Just need to find a diaper." Soon a lady reaches out for me. It's This Lady. I remember her now, too.

She lays me down on a couch, pulls down my pants, and unfastens my diaper. There's stuff everywhere. She starts to wipe my bottom and I start to howl.

"He's going to need a bath," she says to Man. "Go run the water in the sink." Man disappears while This Lady strips me of the rest of my clothes and carries me into the kitchen.

Warm water hits my bottom and I howl louder. I can't help it. It hurts so bad. This Lady's hands move fast over my body before I'm wrapped up in a towel. I'm glad that part is over but I'm still howling.

She puts the white cream all over my bottom before she puts a diaper and new clothes on me. She lays me down on the floor and walks away. Now that my bottom is settled, the ache in my belly is my biggest new problem.

Why is there always another problem waiting for me?

This problem doesn't last long, because This Lady comes back with a bottle. She picks me up and I reach my hands out to grab it. I can hardly breathe and suck it down as fast as I can.

I learned how to hold my own bottle a long time ago. Before that, my mom would bring a bottle and prop it up against my blanket, and then she would leave. Having an aching belly and waiting for a bottle wasn't fun. Having a bottle right next to me and not being able to hold it was horrible. After a while, I learned to hold it myself. Somebody had to hold it; might as well be me! When it was all gone, I liked to hold it in my hands and make noise by banging it on the side of my crib. Here's how it would go: Hit … Noise … Hit … Noise … Hit … Noise. Sometimes I did that for a long, long time.

When the bottle is empty, This Lady burps me and sets me down. As soon as my bottom hits the floor, I fall straight back and land on my head with a big *thud*. I don't cry though. I'm used to stuff hurting.

"You're a tough little thing," This Lady says as she leans down toward me, grabs my hands, and pulls me forward. She lets go, and I start to fall back again, but she catches me first. Whew! That was close.

"What's the matter, Buddy? Don't you know how to sit up?" This Lady is talking to me. I'm sure of it. She's looking right at me and there's no one else around. I *love* when people talk to me.

I watch her face closely, but that's about all I do. I'm not sure if I should smile. I have to think about this because I don't know what she is expecting. I don't know how to do or say much, at least not with words that big people can understand.

The thing is, when I was with my mom, I spent lots of time in my seat or my crib while my mom spent lots of time sleeping or doing things with the men that came to see her. Sometimes I lay for hours, just staring up at the ceiling and turning my head from side to side. I liked the way it felt when it rubbed against my bed and besides, it made a neat sound. Back and forth, back and forth, *swish swish* my head would go until I got tired and fell asleep.

I didn't spend all my time in my crib or seat, though. My mom always took me with her when she went places. Sometimes we went on a bus and she'd hold me in her lap and I liked that the best. I could look at the faces of people on the bus or out the window at all kinds of things passing by.

Sometimes we went in a car and she put me in my seat, which I didn't like as much. It's hard to see things when you're stuck in a seat like mine. All you get to look at is pretty much just the back of the car seat or sometimes the ceiling. Either way, there's not much to see. Being in a car was still a lot better than lying in my crib, though.

Every once in a while, my mom would go next door and give me to the ladies who lived there. That was the best. I *loved* it when she took me there. Sometimes I would sit in a chair with a tray in front of me and I could see all kinds of things going on. People came and went from this place too, but they were mostly kids who talked and played with me. This one time I sat in the chair with the tray and I threw my bottle on the ground. A little girl picked it up and gave it to me. So I threw it again. And she picked it up *again* and we did that so many times it made us both laugh. The next day when I was in my crib, I threw my bottle over the edge to see if my mom would come and pick it up, but nobody came.

I wonder if This Lady will give my bottle back if I throw it. Right now, I'm still watching her face and holding onto her fingers. She doesn't smile at me and I don't smile at her. I let her fingers go, and soon I'm lying back on the floor again, looking up at a ceiling I've never seen before. This Lady walks away and she takes my bottle with her so I have nothing to do but it doesn't bother me.

Suddenly I'm very sleepy and everything fades away as my eyes close.

I wake up to a loud ringing noise and I hear Man's voice. I must have rolled over because I'm on my belly now and the space under my cheek is soggy. I have these two bumps in my mouth. I think two more bumps are coming. My mouth aches.

"Hold on a second," Man says into the phone. "She's around here somewhere." His voice gets louder. "Mama, phone's for you. It's the worker." This Lady appears and takes the phone from his hand.

When she's finished, she comes over to me and picks me up off the floor. She smells my bottom and looks in the back of my diaper. There's nothing there.

"When are you going to get that crib put together?" This Lady asks Man.

"So he's gonna stay? For how long? I thought we were done with this," Man says.

"Todd said he was in court this morning and the judge ordered the baby to stay in foster care. He'll probably need a place for a while," This Lady says.

"And we're gonna be that foster home? This is what you want then? You want to keep him?" Man doesn't sound happy.

"Not exactly, but he's an easy baby. Besides, where's he going to go?" This Lady asks. "Let's just keep him for a few weeks and see what happens."

"There's always gonna be another foster home. They'll find a place. Always do."

"I guess," This Lady says as she looks at me. "A new worker is supposed to come out next week. Maybe they'll have someone lined up by then."

"I doubt it. So I guess you want that crib up now?"

"Sure do, so get to it," This Lady says. Man disappears and This Lady sets me back down on the floor before I hear her footsteps walk away.

I roll my head back and forth, back and forth and listen for the *swish swish* sound.

CHAPTER 4

I LIKE EGGS THE BEST. I like eating them and playing with them. I'm not sure which I like more.

I never ate eggs before I came to live with Man and This Lady, but now I have them almost every morning. I sit in a high chair in the kitchen and This Lady puts eggs on my tray. They are all cut up and warm and squishy in my hands. The first few times I had eggs, I couldn't get them to my mouth by myself, so This Lady had to put them on a spoon and feed me. She always left some on my tray and eventually, with lots of practice, I learned how to pick them up with my hands and feed myself.

I am sitting in my high chair with my eggs when the doorbell rings. This Lady leaves the kitchen and I hear the front door open and close.

"Come on in," This Lady says. "I guess you're from the county?"

This Lady walks into the kitchen with another lady trailing behind her.

"Yes, we spoke on the phone. I'm Dawn, the new caseworker," the new lady says. I stop playing with my eggs.

"Well, it's about time. I expected you three weeks ago. Todd said a new worker would be out within a week. I was wondering when someone was going to show up."

"There was some confusion in our office about who would be assigned to this case. My supervisor gave it to a new worker, but the new worker quit, and so it sat unassigned. But I'm here now," Dawn says.

"So, this must be …" Dawn's voice trails off as she opens a thick binder in her hands and shuffles through lots of papers.

"We call him Buddy," This Lady says. She looks kind of mad. I don't know why.

The thing about This Lady is, she gets mad, but only for a tiny bit and then she's not mad anymore. Sometimes her voice sounds mad even if she's really not. When I throw my eggs on the floor, she uses her mad voice and I don't do it again. Until the next day. Even though her voice sounds mad, she smiles at me sometimes. I always smile back at her.

This Lady might stay mad at Dawn. I'm not sure yet.

"Oh, okay. Forgive me. The office is flooded with cases and sometimes it's hard to keep track of them all. I got four new cases this past week. They just keep coming. Anyway, how's it going with Buddy?" Dawn walks toward me and her face comes low to mine. She scrunches her nose and smiles. I think she's funny and I smile back at her. She seems to like that.

"It's going fine, I guess," This Lady says as she takes a kitchen rag and wipes my face and hands. I *hate* when she does that. I try to squirm away, but there's nowhere to go.

"Has he been back to the doctor?" Dawn is flipping through the pile of papers she has in her hands. "It says here that he was supposed to be seen by now for a follow up on his diaper rash as well as a full well-baby check."

"I took him down to the clinic last week. His bottom has cleared up pretty good. They didn't have shot records for him so he had the first bunch. Let's go sit in the living room." This Lady lifts me out of my high chair and puts me on her hip. She walks down the hall with Dawn and all of her papers.

"Have a seat," This Lady waves her hand toward the couch. We all sit down. I sit on This Lady's lap.

I like to sit on her lap. Her hands have taken care of me since I've been here. They feed me, change me, take me places, put me in my crib at night and get me out of it in the morning. Sometimes Man does, too, but not very often. This Lady's hands are the hands I know.

"Before I forget to ask, does he have a Guardian Ad Litem—you know, that court person who's supposed to come out and check on him?"

"I'm sure he has one, but I don't know who it is. You can call their office and I'm sure they'd look it up and tell you. How was his doctor's appointment?" Dawn asks. She pulls out a pen and pad of paper.

"He has some developmental delays. Todd said he put in a referral for a developmental assessment before he transferred the case, but I haven't heard from anyone. I thought someone would be calling to schedule a time to come out and see him. Why hasn't anyone called? He's been here almost a month."

This Lady doesn't sound happy. She might get mad and stay mad.

"I'll have to check and see," Dawn says as she writes. "He looks like a happy baby." Dawn reaches her hand out to me and I reach back to grab it. I try to put it in my mouth, but she yanks it away. Now she looks mad.

What did she think was going to happen? This is what I don't get about grown-ups. One minute they're smiling and then they aren't. It's hard to keep up.

"He's a good baby," This Lady says. "Sometimes you hardly know he's here, thank goodness. I wouldn't be able to keep up if he wasn't."

"That's good," Dawn says.

"Do you have any idea how long he'll be here?"

"Are you asking for him to be removed?" Dawn asks.

"I didn't say that. I just want to have some idea of how long I should plan for him to be here." This Lady sounds kind of mad again.

"We have the name of a cousin as a possible placement." Dawn shuffles through her papers again and one falls to the floor. "We need to run a background check and make a home visit. If the cousin clears, we'll move Buddy to her."

"Any idea when that might be?" This Lady asks.

"It's hard to say. It depends on how long it takes to get the background checks completed. I'm going to try and make a home visit next week if I can fit it in my schedule. I'd say within a month or so."

"What about visits?" This Lady asks.

"With Mom?" Dawn asks.

"With Mom, Dad, anybody. Is he going to have weekly visits with anyone? I just want to know what to expect. I don't like it when caseworkers call up here out of the blue and tell me I have to have a child ready to go on a visit later that day. That drives me crazy. I have a life, you know. I should get more than a few hours' notice when my day's about to be turned upside-down."

"Well, that's part of being a foster parent. You're required to have the child available when requested." I look from one to the other. Dawn is not smiling. This Lady is not smiling. I'm not smiling either.

"That attitude is why there aren't enough foster parents for all these kids," This Lady says. She's mad now. I'm sure of it.

"There are currently no visits scheduled," Dawn says coolly. "We don't know where Mom is and all we have on the dad is a name without any other information. We're trying to track him down. If something should change, I will let you know." I'm pretty sure Dawn is mad, too.

"Thank you. If you do schedule any visits, I'd appreciate it if you'd give me some notice ahead of time. Like more than a couple of hours," This Lady says.

"I'll do my best," Dawn responds. She gathers her papers, stuffs them into her binder, and stands up. "I always do." She says that so quietly, I barely hear it. This Lady picks me up and stands, too.

"I'll let you know what I find out about his developmental assessment. You can expect to hear from me by the end of the week," Dawn says.

"And I'll let you know if anyone calls to schedule it," This Lady tells her.

"I'd appreciate that. Thank you," Dawn says.

"You're welcome," This Lady says. I think they are both still mad. This Lady opens the front door and Dawn walks out. This Lady shuts the door once Dawn is out of sight.

"Glad she's gone!" This Lady smiles and I smile, too. She's not mad anymore.

A week later, I'm sitting in my high chair while Man makes airplane noises and feeds me my eggs. He looks funny when he opens his mouth wide. I like this game. I wish we played it every day.

This Lady has been busy walking back and forth between the living room and the room where I sleep. Her feet move fast. I can tell by her footsteps.

I wake up from my morning nap when the doorbell rings. I hear Man say hello while This Lady reaches into my crib and pulls me out. She doesn't say a word while she changes my diaper. She usually doesn't talk to me but for some reason, this feels different.

She carries me into the living room where Man is standing with a woman I've never seen before. She smiles at This Lady and me.

"Hi, I'm Melissa, an intern with Children's Services. I'm here to get Buddy. Is he ready to go?" she asks.

"Where's Dawn?" This Lady asks. "When she called this morning to tell me you all would be moving him to a relative, I assumed she'd be the one placing him there. She didn't say she'd be sending someone else."

"Dawn had an emergency and she couldn't make it. I'm just helping her out." Melissa smiles widely.

"Are you a caseworker?" This Lady asks.

"No. I'm still in school. I'm doing an internship at Children's Services this semester." Her smile gets bigger.

"You're a college intern?" This Lady seems surprised.

"Well, yes, but ... it's a little different. It's a paid internship. Most aren't paid," Melissa explains. This Lady just stares at her.

"So Children's Services is paying interns without college degrees to do social work?" This Lady asks.

"Well, um, no, not exactly. A foundation actually pays for the internship."

This Lady keeps looking at her like she should be saying more, so she does.

"They wanted to help Children's Services in some way, so they pay interns to work with and learn from caseworkers. So mostly I just do whatever a caseworker tells me to do. Anyway, I'm here to get Buddy and take him to his mom's cousin. At least I think Dawn said it was a cousin." Her words tumble out fast and all run together. This Lady keeps looking at her but doesn't say anything.

"Is this all his stuff?" Melissa asks, eyeing four large plastic bags lined up along the wall next to my car seat.

"Yes, three of these are his clothes and things. The last one has diapers, wipes, formula, and the rest of the medicated cream he came with for a diaper rash. That's cleared up now, but I included it just in case he needs it," This Lady says. I'm on her hip and I rest my head on her shoulder.

"I'll help you out to your car with these," says Man as he picks up two of the bags and opens the front door. Melissa picks up the other two and they walk outside together.

This Lady holds me tight and puts one of her hands on my head. Her warm finger rests on the tip of my ear. She doesn't say a word as she rocks back and forth just a little bit.

"I'm so glad you have a car seat," Melissa says to Man as they walk back up the steps. "I didn't even think about that!"

"It's the one he came with," Man says. "We washed the cover and tried to air it out, but it still smells like smoke."

"He's getting a little big for it," says This Lady. She kisses me on the forehead, bends over, puts me in my seat, and fastens the belt. She stands up straight and turns to Melissa.

"Do you have any questions about him? Do you know he has another check-up at the clinic in two weeks? Do you need the date and time for that appointment?"

"You can tell me, but Dawn said not to worry about any of that. She said the information is in the file," Melissa responds.

"Don't you want to know what formula he is on? He just started solid foods. Don't you want to know about that?"

"Oh, yes, of course," Melissa says as she looks at a phone she holds in her hand. "I really have to go, though, so maybe you could just call Dawn and let her know?" She puts her phone in her pocket and lifts me up, along with my seat.

"Never mind," This Lady says. "Just give me the name and number of the relative and I'll call her myself."

"I'm not allowed to give that out." Melissa shakes her head slowly. "But I can give her your information and she can contact you if she wants to." Everything freezes. It's quiet and still in the room until Man moves.

"Here's his diaper bag." He hands Melissa the same diaper bag I've always had. Suddenly, I'm glad to be in the seat I know, even if it smells.

"Okay, great, well, thank you for everything," Melissa says. "Maybe I'll see you again on another case." She sounds very nice.

"I doubt that," This Lady says. "We retired before we took him. We're going to stay retired this time."

Man leans over and puts his hand on my belly.

"Good-bye, Buddy. You be a good boy." He smiles at me and I smile at him, even though my belly aches with emptiness. This Lady leans down, too, and kisses my cheek. Then she turns away.

Melissa puts my diaper bag on her shoulder, lifts the handle of my pumpkin seat and carries me out the front door and down to the street. My seat knocks against her knees as she shifts from one hand to the other. I roll my head back and forth, back and forth. Somehow, it makes me feel better.

She loads me into her car and backs out of the driveway. From where I sit, I can see Man and This Lady standing on the porch. This Lady waves to me as we drive away.

All at once, the hands I know are gone.

It's time for Something Next.

CHAPTER 5

<small>MELISSA IS A TALKER.</small>

I love that! Somehow it helps the rumbles in my belly feel better.

"So, little Buddy, how ya doing back there?" I can't see her, but I feel her hand reach back into my seat and touch my head. "You're awful cute, you know."

Of course, I don't talk back to her. There are a few things I can do instead. I can cry. I can scream. I can screech, and I can laugh, but I don't do any of those things right now.

"We're on our way to Gloria's house. She's your mom's cousin. I think that's what Dawn said. Anyhow, you are related. You're going to live with her now. We should be there soon. How about some music? What do you like to listen to?" Melissa says. "Hmm, nothing? Well, we should try to lay off the X-rated stuff. Let's see what we can find." Her hand is no longer on my head and I hear music. I haven't heard sounds like that since I lived with my mom, but her music was loud and hurt my ears. Melissa's music isn't too loud. It's happy.

A little while later, the car stops and so does the music. Melissa gets out and taps on the window beside me so I turn my head to see her smiling and waving. She's silly. I smile back and she opens the door. She lifts me and my seat out of the car and shuts the door with her foot. She looks up a long flight of concrete steps.

"Wow, that's a lot of steps. I guess this is my exercise for today. You're heavy, at least you plus this seat!" she says. One by one she climbs the steps with my seat knocking against her knees. It's a bumpy ride.

She sets me down on the porch and knocks on the front door. There are lots of voices coming from inside, but no one answers. She knocks harder and louder. The door swings open.

"Come in," a lady says as she steps to the side to make way for Melissa and me and my seat.

"Are you Gloria?" Melissa asks. She looks around the room and so do I. There's a lot to take in.

An old woman with gray hair sits on a saggy couch next to a man and a teenager leans against a doorframe. His arms are crossed and he doesn't move. No one else does, either. It's suddenly very quiet.

"Yeah, that's me," says the lady who opened the door.

"Hi, I'm Melissa from Children's Services. This is Buddy. I'm supposed to place him with you today." She sets me and my seat on the ground. Melissa's smile and silliness are suddenly gone.

"Yeah, I know. Dawn called earlier and told me you'd be bringing him."

Melissa bends over and unfastens the straps of my car seat. She lifts me up and puts me on her hip.

"He's a really good baby. Very sweet," Melissa tells her.

"I've only seen him once, when my cousin dropped him off here for a couple nights back when he was a newborn. She only calls when she needs something," Gloria says.

"Would you like to hold him? I need to bring his things in from the car," Melissa says. Gloria doesn't say anything but holds out her hands.

"I'll be right back." Melissa disappears and returns with two trash bags, one in each hand. She sets them on the floor without saying anything and comes back a second time with the other two trash bags, plus my diaper bag.

"This is everything," Melissa says.

"Does he come with a voucher for clothes and stuff?" Gloria asks as she shifts me from one hip to the other. Her hips are bony. I'm not very comfortable.

"I don't think so. It looks like he has everything he needs. The foster parents sent a lot of stuff. You can ask Dawn about a voucher if there's something you need for him that he doesn't already have."

"What about WIC vouchers?" Gloria asks. Melissa looks even more confused.

"I don't know anything about WIC vouchers. Dawn would have to answer that. You can call her. Do you have her number?"

"It's on my phone," Gloria says. "I'll get in touch with her."

"Oh here, I almost forgot." Melissa pulls a small piece of paper out of her coat pocket. "Here's the name and number of his former foster parents. They'd be happy to talk to you or answer any of your questions about Buddy if you want to call them. They'd probably be able to tell you more than Dawn anyway," Melissa says.

"Tony, come get this piece of paper. I have my hands full." The boy from the doorway walks forward and Melissa smiles and hands him the paper. He looks down and doesn't smile at her.

"Okay, well, I'm going to head on my way," Melissa says as she walks to the door. Her voice trails off and her hand lingers on the door knob. She has a look on her face, but I don't know what it is. It's not happy or sad, but I don't think it's a good one.

"Thanks for bringing him," Gloria says. With that, the door shuts and Melissa is gone.

The ache in my belly is back.

"Mama, I don't know why I let you talk me into this," Gloria says as she walks toward the old woman who sits in the chair. "You know I don't need those welfare people all up in my business and in my house."

Gloria dumps me into the old lady's lap. Her hands are cold and wrinkles cut deep lines in her face. And her breath stinks. Yuck!

"You already have people in your business and in your house. Tony's probation officer is here every few weeks," Wrinkles says.

"Ma, here's the paper the lady gave me." Tony holds out the piece of paper Melissa had given to him. Gloria turns to the boy and snatches the paper from him.

"If you wouldn't go beating up on people and skipping school, I wouldn't have to worry about that, either," Gloria says to the boy. Her words are fast and harsh. She crumples up the paper and throws it into the kitchen.

"People get what they deserve," Tony says. His words are harsh,

29

too. The man on the couch laughs.

"Ain't that right? Boy's got a point," he says.

"The boy's got two assault charges and his head up his ass. He's gonna end up in lockdown if he don't get it together." I think Gloria is mad. Maybe all these people are mad.

"Chill," the man says. "The kid is thirteen. They don't want him in lockdown any more than he wants to be there."

"If he keeps it up, I'll be putting him in lockdown myself." Gloria's words whip through the air and the man laughs again. "The last thing I need is to raise another one right up behind him."

"So you'd rather just give your cousin's baby to strangers to raise? That ain't the way family works. He belongs to us, like it or not," Wrinkles says.

I sit on Wrinkles' lap in my soggy, squishy diaper while they throw more words around the room and my belly gurgles. Although I don't want to, I can't help but start to cry.

"He's probably hungry," Wrinkles says. "Here, take him and I'll make him a bottle." Nobody moves.

"You heard her, Tony. Take that baby," Gloria says. Tony picks me up from Wrinkles' lap and holds me under my arms as far away from his body as he can. Wrinkles moves slowly and walks over to the trash bags that came with me.

"This kid stinks," Tony says. He hands me to Gloria. She carries me over to the bags, digs through them until she finds a diaper, and lays me down on the floor to change it. I feel a tickle up my arm.

"Damn roaches," Gloria says as her hand brushes against my arm and a little brown thing flies across the floor.

I return to Wrinkles' lap for my bottle and try to ignore her smelly breath. I drink my bottle down quick, desperate to ease the ache in my belly. It doesn't help, though, and minutes later, the stuff from my bottle comes back up and splatters onto Wrinkles' shirt and down the side of the chair.

"He's a spitter," Wrinkles says. "Grab me a towel or something." Gloria digs through my trash bags and pulls out a burp cloth. It's the same one This Lady used to use all the time. I'm happy to see it.

Wrinkles wipes my face, her shirt, and the chair. My shirt is soggy, but I don't care. I just want everything to go away.

It's time to pull my disappearing act. I'm so glad I mastered that trick when I lived with my mom.

I close my eyes and before I know it, everything fades away.

When I wake up, my face is pressed against soft white mesh and over and over again, something wet moves across my cheek. It startles me. I jerk and lift my head up to get a better look.

I'm not sure what it is, but it is white and brown and furry and has four legs. Something on the back of it sticks up high in the air and moves back and forth really fast. I watch it for a long time.

"Alex, leave that baby alone," Gloria calls from the other room. The thing disappears. I wish it didn't. I like it, even if I don't know what it is.

Gloria comes into the room, bends over me, lifts me up, and carries me into the kitchen.

The thing is there again, sitting on the floor and staring up at me.

"Tony, come get this dog. I don't know where you picked up this stray, but you better keep it away from this baby. I don't want to be responsible for him getting hurt."

"Alex, come girl," Tony calls from the other room, but Alex doesn't move.

"Well, let's see what kind of food you can eat," Gloria says as she puts me in a high chair. "What about macaroni and cheese?"

She puts a pile of yellow slimy stuff on the tray and walks away. I'm glad I learned how to get food to my mouth when I lived with Man and This Lady. Even though Gloria disappears, Alex sits beside me on the floor, staring up at me with big brown eyes and floppy brown ears. I eat and play with my macaroni and when I'm done, I drop some on the floor by Alex and it falls right on her big, pink tongue. For the first time since I got here, I smile.

Alex's happy eyes follow my every move, so I drop some more

macaroni for her. This time, it lands on her back. She turns her head from one side to the other trying to reach it and then starts walking in circles. It is so funny, I laugh. She stops and looks up at me with her floppy ears, so I throw some more. We play this game for a long, long time.

Eventually, Gloria returns. She doesn't say a word as she lifts me out of the high chair.

"Shoo, dog. Go away," she says as waves her hand in front of Alex. Her angry voice returns. I don't make any noise.

Gloria changes my diaper and carries me into the living room. Alex is curled up in my car seat. I've never seen anyone or anything else in my car seat before!

"Get out of that seat," Gloria orders as Alex jumps out of it and I am put into it. Gloria walks away again, but Alex curls up on the floor beside me. I reach over and tug on her ear. She lifts her head up and wiggles it. I pull it some more and she licks me. When I make noise with my mouth, her ears go up. When I'm quiet, they go down. I can't believe I can make this happen.

We play until both of us fall sound asleep.

CHAPTER 6

LIVING IN GLORIA'S HOUSE MAKES my ears hurt. It makes my belly hurt, too. Actually, it makes all of me hurt.

There are two times when I don't hurt. First, when I'm sleeping. Second, when Alex stays close beside me. When Alex is with me, which is most of the time, I still hurt, but not as much. Just having Alex with me makes me feel better.

I usually fall asleep anywhere at night and in the morning, I wake up in my bed. It's not really a bed, though. I think it's a play pen. It's the greatest place in the world, because Alex sleeps with me. Well, maybe not *really* with me, but it's all just the same because she sleeps on the ground on the other side of the white mesh.

I wake up in the morning and the yelling has already started. Alex's ears perk up for a moment, then she lays her head between her two front paws on the floor.

"Tony, get your ass out of bed!"

Gloria screams at Tony all the time. Maybe it doesn't hurt his ears, though, because he doesn't seem to hear her. It only makes her scream louder and louder until he starts yelling, too. Alex and I stay quiet.

"You can't make me do shit," he growls. Tony emerges from his bedroom and stands eye-to-eye with his mom. She smacks him hard across the face.

"Get the hell out of my house and go to school!" The words bounce around the room, off the walls, and land with a deafening thud in my belly. Lots of times, I feel just a little bit … yuck. Tony storms out the door and it slams behind him.

I don't know how Wrinkles sleeps through all this ruckus, but most of the time, she is in bed. Maybe she's just pretending to be asleep. Sometimes I do that, too. It's easier that way.

Not everybody sleeps in a bed here. There's always someone sleeping on the couch. Usually it's one of the two men who were here on the first day I came. They look the same to me and they always wear the same clothes—white T-shirts and jeans.

Just after Tony storms out the door, I hear a knock. The knocking lasts for a long time while Gloria rushes around the living room with the man. They shove some things under the couch and put other things in other rooms while the knocking gets louder and louder. Gloria scoops me up from the floor and puts me on her hip. She sticks her finger in her mouth then rubs back and forth on my chin. She does this several times. Crusty stuff flakes off into the air.

Alex follows us as Gloria walks over to the door and holds it open. Alex barks, but Gloria doesn't say anything. It's Dawn, the lady with all the papers who came to see me when I lived with Man and This Lady.

"Is the dog friendly?" Dawn asks. She doesn't move.

"She won't hurt you," Gloria says. Alex sits at Gloria's feet. Her barking has stopped. Dawn steps inside.

"You must be Gloria," she says as she holds out her hand. Gloria shakes it. "It's nice to finally meet you. You're a tough lady to get a hold of. I've left messages for you but haven't heard back."

"What messages? I only got one," Gloria says.

"I've left several since Buddy arrived in your home last month."

"He ain't even been here a month," Gloria says. "More like a couple weeks." Dawn shakes her head and pulls out a piece of paper and shows it to Gloria. "Oh, I guess it has been that long. Come to think of it, it does feel like he's been here forever. Here, have a seat."

Wrinkles shuffles into the room as Dawn sits down. She holds her bony, cold hands out to Gloria.

"I'll take him," she says. Wrinkles heads toward her chair and as she sits, I settle down into her lap. My soggy diaper goes *swish, swish* but I'm the only one who knows it. Maybe that's because I'm the only one who *feels* it. Alex trots over and sniffs it. Maybe she knows, too. Wrinkles shoos her away, but Alex ignores her and sits down at Wrinkles' feet.

"How is everything?" Dawn asks.

"Real good," Wrinkles says with a big smile. Dawn smiles, too.

"How's Buddy doing?" Dawn turns to Gloria and waits for her answer.

"He's doin' real good. Aren't you, Buddy? You're so happy. Yes, you are!" She reaches out for me and Wrinkles hands me over.

I don't know what I'm supposed to do, because I've never heard Gloria's voice sound like this. Usually, she's yelling.

All eyes are on me and Gloria. I don't move.

"Come on, now," she continues as her fingers tickle my belly. "Where's my big boy's smile?"

I have no idea what she is doing. She's never talked to me like this before. She never talks to me at all and she doesn't touch me unless she has to. I don't know what to do or if I'm supposed to do anything.

For whatever reason, the adults start to giggle. I don't know why, though. Maybe they are all crazy. Even Dawn.

I guess if they giggle, it's good. If they stay happy, maybe Gloria won't start yelling again.

"So, today's a big day. Do you have any plans?" Dawn asks. Wrinkles and Gloria stare at each other.

"What do you mean, a big day?"

"It's Buddy's first birthday. I was going through my mail at my office this morning and noticed his date of birth on a form from the court."

"Oh, it's his birthday? We had no idea. Well, whadda ya know about that?" Gloria lifts me high in the air and smiles at me. As I go up, my belly does too and spills its contents onto Gloria's shoulder. Oops.

I can't help it. My belly does whatever it wants to. Sometimes I spit up after I eat and sometimes stuff comes back up for no good reason. Other times, my belly gurgles and a sludge of yuck fills my diaper and burns my bottom. Other times, my belly is rock hard and big and full and nothing comes out of anywhere.

"Mama, get me something to wipe this up," Gloria screams. Wrinkles reaches over and pats Gloria's shoulder with a rag.

"You didn't know it was his birthday?" Dawn asks.

"How would I know that?" Gloria responds. "It's not like he can tell me, and Erica certainly don't come around to tell me nothin'."

"It should be on the paperwork that was left with you on the day he came to live here. Speaking of which, has he been to the clinic? He was behind on shots and he's due for a well-baby check, too," Dawn explains.

"Yeah, I been calling that place but can never get through. Have to wait on hold for hours. Who has time for that?"

"He needs to be seen," Dawn says. "Have you heard from your cousin at all?"

"Erica? No. She ain't called a single time and she probably ain't gonna. She got a warrant out on her."

Dawn pulls out two small cards and hands one to Gloria and one to Wrinkles.

"If you talk to her, please give her my name and number." Gloria hands her card to Wrinkles.

"Will do," Wrinkles says. Dawn stands up to leave.

"Oh, I almost forgot to ask. Have you met Buddy's GAL?" Dawn asks.

"What's a GAL?"

"GAL stands for *guardian ad litem*. It's the person who represents Buddy's best interest in court. He or she … usually a she, not many men in this line of work … anyway, she is supposed to visit Buddy and make recommendations to the judge about what is best for him."

"Why does he need a GAL if he has you? Isn't that your job?" Gloria seems annoyed.

"No. My job is to serve the whole family. The GAL only serves the best interest of the child."

Gloria doesn't respond. She looks like she's bored with the entire conversation.

"You should be hearing from the GAL soon." Dawn bends over me and pats me on the head.

"Happy Birthday, Buddy! I hope you have a wonderful day."
The front door closes behind her.
I pull my disappearing trick and everything disappears.

CHAPTER 7

I can roll over now. It's my new trick. I'm glad I learned it, because there's a lot more to look at than just the ceiling most of the time. Like Alex.

Alex is my favorite part of everything and much more interesting to watch than the ceiling. I used to have to move my head and body all around so I could see what she was doing. I did that so much that one day I rolled right over onto my belly and everything looked different. Well, I guess Alex looked the same. The same silly tongue and big brown eyes and floppy ears. I try to eat those ears. They don't taste very good, but I like trying to eat them anyway. Alex might not have hands, but she makes me feel as good as I did when Maggie's hands held me on the night my mom ran away. Sometimes, when I fall asleep on the floor, Alex lays her head across my feet. As soon as I wake up, her ears perk up and she nuzzles her nose in my hand.

There are a lot of hands in this house. First, there's Gloria's hands. They are harsh and fast, a spark of fire just under the surface threatening to ignite. When her hands touch me, I feel like I'm teetering on the edge of disaster. So far, I've avoided it.

Wrinkles' hands are cold and bony, but they don't sizzle with rage like Gloria's. I'm glad they're here because they are useful, like when I need to eat or need a diaper change.

I spend time in Tony's hands, too. So far, those are the best hands I've felt. They are also the only hands that pet Alex, rub her ears and scratch her belly. Alex likes Tony's hands, so I like them, too. I don't like when Tony yells, but he only does that when Gloria yells at him first.

Sometimes, I get passed between the hands of men who visit and sit on the couch while other visitors come and go. The front door opens and closes all day long, so much that someone just yells "Come in!" whenever anybody knocks.

The thing I like about one of the men is he talks to me sometimes. He's the only one who does. It's nice to be seen, even if I don't talk back. He doesn't kick Alex off the couch, either, when she jumps up to sit with us.

He and I are sitting on the couch when someone knocks on the door for the third time today.

"Come in!" He doesn't move. Neither to do I. Nobody comes. The knock continues.

"I said come in!" he yells again. The hinges on the door creak and a head pops around the door frame.

"I'm looking for Michael Wilson," the mouth on the head says.

"Ain't nobody here by that name," he says. "You best move along."

"Is this the home of Gloria Reynolds?" The head is still in the door frame.

"Yeah, that be my cousin. She ain't here. What you want with her anyway?" he says. The head is attached to a body. Arms push the door open and a lady steps inside.

"My name is Diane Beckman. I'm the *guardian ad litem* appointed to represent Michael Wilson in court."

The man just looks at her. The lady keeps talking.

"It's my understanding that he is living at this address in the care of his mother's cousin, Gloria Reynolds. Would this, by chance, be Michael?" She is looking at me.

"This here's Buddy," he says as he pats my leg. "That's what we call him. I don't know him by any other name."

"Is Buddy's mom named Erica?" she asks.

"Yeah, that be my other cousin," he says.

"So, you're related to both Gloria and Erica?" He nods.

"What's your name?" she asks.

"You can call me Squid," he says.

"Is that your name?"

"That's what everybody calls me."

HOLLY SCHLAACK

"What's your real name?"

"You mean my government name?"

"I mean your legal name. The one on your Social Security card."

"Why you need to know that? You ain't coming to see me. You coming to see Gloria."

"Well, I am coming to see Gloria, but I'm also here to see the baby. I'm asking you for your name because we need to run a background check. Anyone who is watching or babysitting for Michael has to be approved."

"For real?" He makes a funny face.

The words go back and forth, but they don't bounce off the walls and no one seems angry.

"For real. It's policy. A while back, there was a case where a child was living with a relative and no one knew it, but the babysitter she was using was a registered sex offender. He raped the little girl."

"That is messed up. People whack." He has another funny look on his face.

"Don't I know it," she says, smiling as she pulls a pen and pad of paper out of her bag. "So, you gonna work with me here or what?"

"Oh yeah. My name is Ronnie Harris. Ronald, I guess. That's the name on my Social Security card," he replies. He rattles off some numbers while she writes.

"Thank you. Do you live here?"

"Naw, I just visit. Help out when I can. Gloria, she got her hands full. She taken care of her mama and Tony be stressin' her out."

"How do you think Buddy is doing here?" I turn my head to look at her when I hear my name.

"This little dude? He doin' fine. We just hangin' out."

It's true. We do just hang out. Mostly I just eat, sleep, sit on the couch, or lay on the floor and play with Alex. Sometimes, when the front door opens and closes, I see it is light outside and I remember when I used to go outside, like with my mom on a bus or with Man and This Lady. I haven't been outside since I got here and the windows are always covered up so no light gets in.

40

Two women come to the door and it creaks open again. A sliver of sunshine cuts across the room.

"I'll holler at y'all later," he calls out and waves them away. They disappear, along with the light.

"So, who all lives here?" Diane asks.

"Just Gloria, her mom, and Tony," he says.

"It's really important that I talk to Gloria. Do you know when she'll be home? What's the best way to reach her?"

"She be back in a couple hours. I think she went to the store. You can call here later tonight if you want. She probably be here then."

"I'm going to leave you my name and number," Diane says as she writes something down and hands it to him. "Please ask her to call me as soon as possible." She stands up, walks toward me, and lowers her face to mine.

"Bye, little guy. I'll see you soon." I watch her as she walks out the front door. She talked to me.

I love that!

CHAPTER 8

I'M GOING OUTSIDE TODAY!

Gloria stuffs me into my car seat, pulling the straps tight across my belly. It smells like home, the place I lived with my mom. I like the old smell, but I don't like how it feels. Everything is tight and I might bust out of it all together.

"How the hell does this thing work?" Gloria asks as she yanks and pushes and pulls the stubborn belts that won't give way. They are as strong as she is and I'm just caught in the middle, wondering who will win and hoping it doesn't hurt too much, whichever way it goes.

"Didn't have car seats for a hundred years. Don't know why we need 'em now," she says. I think she's talking to herself. Finally, she gives up and throws a blanket over me in my seat.

She leaves my seat in the car and carries me into a big building with lots of people. There are tons of kids there, some the same size as me. I've never seen so many kids in one place before. My eyes take in everything from the kids to the bright colors on the walls to the stuff that sits on shelves and tables. I've never seen so many things before.

We wait for a long time. I stay very quiet while I sit on Gloria's lap.

"He's adorable. How old is he?" asks a lady sitting near us. She has someone the same size as me siting on her lap, too.

"He turned a year a couple months back," Gloria responds.

"She did, too! Isn't that right, Princess?" The baby looks up at the lady who is holding her and reaches up to touch her face. They are both smiling until the baby starts to squirm. Something falls and slides across the floor.

"Uh-oh," Princess says as she looks down.

"You dropped your book. Pick it up," the lady says. She sets Princess down and Princess *walks*. She bends over and with both hands, she picks something up off the floor. When she stands up, she looks at me.

I've never seen someone so little walk. I can't do that. How does she know how? I can't believe it. I can't take my eyes off her.

She walks toward me and holds out her hands.

"Book," she says. I just look at her. She says it again. Then she throws it at me but not very hard and it doesn't hurt.

This kid says words, too. Unbelievable!

"Princess! We don't throw books. I'm sorry. She's just being friendly. She's always wants to share. I figure I better enjoy that now. It won't be long before she won't want to share anything. You know how they get when the 'terrible twos' set in," the lady says to Gloria. She picks up the book and holds it out to me. I don't know what to do. Gloria reaches out and takes it.

"Oh, that's alright. He don't mind." She's right. I don't mind. Gloria puts the book in my hands and I grab it. It's hard to hold, but I don't drop it. It's squishy in my hands. I've never touched something like this before.

"This one is always running around. Wears me out." The lady stands up and chases Princess, who is giggling and looking back at us as she moves away. The lady scoops her up and turns back to us. "He sits so nicely. Princess doesn't do that much unless she's really tired. Or sick. Is your little guy sick?"

"No, he ain't sick. He's just a good baby." Gloria's right. I'm not sick. I am a good baby, but I can't run around and say words like this little girl.

"That's us," Gloria says as she stands, after a loud voice calls out. Gloria hands the book back to the lady. She waves at me.

"Bye bye," she says. Princess does the same thing. Unbelievable!

We follow the lady with the loud voice back to a small room. She asks Gloria some questions as Gloria takes off my clothes and sets me on a cold, hard metal thing.

"Hmmm, it looks like he hasn't gained much weight since he was here a few months ago," the lady says.

"I don't know why. He eats plenty," Gloria tells her.

That's not exactly true. Mostly, I still have bottles, and sometimes whatever is in them doesn't taste very good. I eat some food when I'm in my high chair, which isn't very often. Sometimes I eat while I'm sitting on the couch with Squid. I've gotten good at getting food to my mouth with my fingers.

There's a knock on the door and another lady enters the room. She's wearing a white coat and is carrying a metal thing with a screen.

"Hello, I'm Dr. Evans," she says as she looks up from the thing in her hands. She holds one hand out toward Gloria and they shake hands. Gloria's other hand is on my naked belly as I lay on a tall table with paper beneath me. It crinkles loudly as I move my head back and forth, back and forth. I like the sound.

"Forgive me if I'm a little slow. We just switched to a new computer system," Dr. Evans says as she taps on the thing in her hands. "It looks like Michael had his first birthday last month."

"That's right, he did," Gloria says. "He has a Nickname. Buddy. Everyone calls him Buddy."

"Well there, Buddy, how are you today?" Dr. Evans looks me in the eye so I look down. Her hands grab mine as she pulls me into a sitting position. She lets go and I start to wobble but I don't fall over all the way. She talks to me the *whole time*. I smile big and show her my two new teeth.

I've gotten better about sitting up all by myself. I couldn't do that when I lived with my mom. I started learning how when I lived with Man and This Lady. I started to forget when I moved to Gloria's and spent so much time on the floor. Being on the floor was good, though, because Alex made me want to learn how to roll over so I could watch her and try to follow her. I can scoot around and I'm getting faster. So by now I can *kind of* sit and I can *kind of* scoot. Maybe someday I'll figure out how to put it all together.

Dr. Evans lays me back on the table and undoes the tabs on my diaper.

"This diaper rash looks pretty bad," she says. "How long has this been going on?"

"Not too long," Gloria says. "I been putting some cream on it. Sometimes it goes away and then comes back."

"It's going to take some work on your part to get it resolved. He's going to need to be changed every couple of hours and spend some time diaper-free. His skin needs fresh air. I'll also prescribe more cream, which will need to be applied at every change."

Dr. Evans does lots more things like listen to my belly, measure my head, and ask Gloria tons of questions.

"Let me show you something," Dr. Evans says, extending the thing in her hands toward Gloria, who moves closer so she can see it.

"This is Buddy's growth chart. From the time he was first seen in the hospital until now, he's grown a tiny bit, but not enough. Ideally, we would have seen a greater increase in both his height and weight. His head should be growing, too. At thirteen months, he should be eating a variety of table foods. Is he still on a bottle?"

"Yeah, he likes his bottle. Almost always has one in his hands. He likes to hold it. He fusses when I take it away."

They talk some more; something about introducing new foods and eating regularly, on a schedule, many times a day.

"You also need to supplement his diet with Pediasure, a drink that is rich in nutrients. It will help give him the nutrition he needs. His brain is growing fast right now, and it needs all the help it can get so he'll be as healthy as possible," Dr. Evans explains.

"That stuff you're talking about, Pediasure, is it covered by Medicaid? I can barely make ends meet, and I don't know that I can add some fancy drink to my monthly bills," Gloria says.

"Yes, it's covered. We'll make sure you have what you need to give him what he needs."

"Oh really? 'Cuz I ain't never had what I need for nothing."

I look at Dr. Evans. I can tell she doesn't know what to say. After a long pause, Dr. Evans speaks.

"Before you leave today, I'll introduce you to Yvonne. She's a social worker here in the clinic, and she can help you. There are a few things we need to arrange. For one, developmental services. By now, Buddy should be at least crawling, pulling up, and getting ready to walk, if not already walking. I haven't heard him say much since you both got here. Does he use any words?"

"He fusses and hollers sometimes, enough to let me know he needs or wants something. Other than that, he don't make a lot of noise. He's easy," Gloria says.

"Easy is not always good," Dr. Evans explains.

"Easy is about all I can do and what I do is good enough," Gloria says.

Dr. Evans doesn't know what to say again. I'm sure of it.

"Okay, well, I'm going to send Yvonne in to talk with you further. Buddy also needs another set of immunizations. It's going to take several extra visits to get him caught up. I'd like to see him back in two weeks to check on his diaper rash and for a weight check."

Gloria looks at her phone.

"How long is it gonna take? I already been here three hours and I gotta go to work." She's mad. I can hear it.

"Yvonne is finishing up with another family now. It shouldn't be long," Dr. Evans says as she reaches her hand out to me. I grab her finger and we trade smiles. She leans over. "You have some growing to do, little guy, and I know you can do it."

The door closes behind her. It's just me and Gloria.

I stay still while on her lap, hoping maybe she will forget that I'm here, that we are here together, and that we have to wait some more. Hoping maybe the sizzle in her hands will disappear like I wish I could.

She abruptly stands with me in her arms and swings the door wide open. It slams against the wall and a bouncy sound echoes down the hall.

"I ain't got time for this. I got to go," she says. I don't know who she is talking to. Maybe no one. I know for sure she is not talking to me.

I am glad.

I don't make a single sound as Gloria stuffs me back me into my car seat and doesn't even try to make the straps go where they are supposed to. I'm pretty big for my seat now, so maybe I don't need the straps as much. As soon as the car starts to move, she pulls out her phone and starts yelling.

"I told you, Erica, I done raised my kids and I ain't doing this anymore. You need to get off them drugs and take care of this kid. He's your responsibility. I don't need this hassle."

Her words go on and on and on and I can't feel her hands but I know they have sizzle.

Flecks of red and blue lights bounce around the car and I hear sirens. I've heard them before. The car slows to a stop. Gloria quickly throws a blanket over me so only my head is sticking out. I close my eyes and use my disappearing trick.

"Good afternoon, ma'am." His voice is deep.

"Good afternoon, officer," Gloria says. She sounds nice. It's a new sound to me.

"Do you have any idea why I stopped you?"

"I have no idea. I'm just on my way home from taking my cousin's little boy to the doctor. He's been real sick."

"Do you need an ambulance?"

"No, sir. Just a virus, that's all. I'm trying to get him home where he'll be comfortable."

"I stopped you because you're driving erratically. You crossed the yellow line several times."

"I did? I'm so sorry. I been sick with worry about this poor little fella and I guess I was distracted."

"Can I see your license, please?" I hear Gloria digging through her bag for a long time. I'm still disappeared.

"Here it is," she says. Footsteps walk away and after a while, they come back.

"I'm giving you a warning this time. It won't help the baby any for you to get so wound up while driving. You get him home and take good care."

"I will, officer. Thank you." Her voice is so nice. I hope it stays that way.

Gloria slams the front door behind us and thrusts me into Wrinkles' arms. Her cold fingers make me shiver.

"You want this kid so bad, you take him!" she says. Her nice voice is gone.

Wrinkles doesn't answer. She shuffles across the floor with me in her arms. We head to the kitchen and she puts me in my seat. Alex sits at my feet, like she always does.

Wrinkles drops some cereal onto my tray and walks away.

I'm not hungry anyway, so I drop the pieces one by one onto Alex's big, pink tongue.

At least I got to go outside today.

CHAPTER 9

THERE'S TWO OF THEM AT the door this time. Tony stumbles toward it and pulls it open. He doesn't say anything to the faces on the other side.

"Hi, Tony. We're here to see Gloria. I'm Diane, the GAL for Buddy, and this is Dawn, Buddy's caseworker from Children's Services."

Tony rubs sleep from his eyes. I rub mine, too. Even Alex barely lifts her head before she drops it back down on the floor between her paws and closes her eyes. We must've fallen asleep on the couch last night. Sometimes that happens.

"Does my mom know you're coming?" Tony asks.

"No," Diane says. "Both of us have been trying to reach her, but she hasn't returned our calls. We decided to take a chance and come out this morning, hoping to catch her. Can we come in?"

Tony holds the door open and they both step inside.

"She's sleeping. You want me to wake her?"

"That would be great," Dawn says. Tony disappears down the hall. I'm more awake now, and I lift my head to get a better look.

"Good morning, Buddy! Did you have a good sleep?" Diane takes two steps toward me. Suddenly, Alex is awake too, and she is not happy. I can tell by her growl. Diane takes two steps back. "On second thought, I'll just stay right here." She and Dawn exchange nervous looks.

"I'm not so sure this early visit was a good idea," Dawn says. Her voice is quiet.

"First of all, it's not that early. It's eight-thirty. Why isn't Tony in school? Second, it's not like she's given us any other option. She never returns calls. What are we supposed to do?" Diane's voice is quiet, too. Alex's head is on the floor again between her paws.

I hear Gloria's feet hit the floor. Here she comes. Oh boy. Diane smiles wide.

"You must be Gloria. I'm Diane, Buddy's GAL."

"And I'm Dawn, his caseworker. We've met before."

Before Gloria can say a word, Diane starts talking again.

"I'm so sorry to disrupt your morning like this. I hate to pop in unannounced, but I've had such a hard time getting a hold of you. I know you're really busy, because every time I call or come by, you're not here. I figured you'd be up and getting Tony off to school. We didn't realize we'd be waking you guys. Is Tony off school today?" Diane's voice is friendly.

"He's sick today." Gloria's arms are folded and her voice is flat.

"He is? I'm sorry to hear that. Poor guy. What does he have? There's a lot of stuff going around right now. Of course, allergies are a problem this time of year, too." Diane turns to face, Tony who is leaning against the wall. "How are you feeling?" she asks him. Tony just coughs.

Gloria picks me up off the couch.

"You all can have a seat," she says. "I got to go change him. I'll be back."

She puts me on her hip and walks out of the room with Alex trailing behind. When we return, I have a clean diaper, clean clothes, and a fresh bottle. Dawn and Diane are sitting on the couch. I don't know where Tony went.

"So, Dawn and I figured if we made a visit together, that would be easier, so you don't have multiple visits to juggle."

"That's fine. I have some questions for you all anyway," Gloria says as she sits down next to Diane. Diane smiles at me and reaches her hand out toward me, so I reach back and she smiles.

"Then I'm glad we are finally all together. First, how is Buddy doing? Do you have any concerns?" Diane asks while I wrap my fingers around one of hers.

"Buddy's fine. He went to the doctor last week and he's not growing a whole lot, so I have to give him some extra drink called Pediasure. He's supposed to go back next week for another check-up."

"Did the doctor say why he isn't growing as much as he should?" Dawn asks. This is the first time she's said anything.

"No, not really. And some lady is supposed to come out here and do a developmental assessment. I got her name and number. I'll call her today."

"I was going to ask you about that," Diane says. "We have a court hearing next week, and I know the judge is going to ask about that. If at all possible, having the assessment done before the hearing would be ideal." Diane turns to Dawn.

"Actually," Dawn says, "I got notice yesterday that the referral was cancelled due to lack of contact with the family. I'll have to get him back on the list."

"Shoot." Diane does not look happy. She turns to Gloria. "Is there a reason you didn't get in touch with them?"

"No, I just been busy. Got a lot goin' on. Besides, I think Buddy's fine. Look at him. Do you see anything wrong with him?"

Dawn and Diane's eyes are on me now. I don't know what they are looking at or looking for, so I let go of Diane's finger and just sit quietly on Gloria's lap. I'm never entirely comfortable here.

"Do you have copies of his medical records?" Diane asks Dawn.

"No. It takes ages to get those. I put in a request, though."

"Well, here's the thing," Diane says to Gloria. "Even if he doesn't have any delays, there's no downside to having an assessment done."

"I can put in another referral," Dawn offers.

"Let's go ahead and do that," Diane says.

"I have some questions for you all. There's a court hearing next week?" Gloria asks. "Do I have to go to that?"

"No, you don't have to go, but it's always helpful if the judge can hear from the person caring for the child," Dawn tells her.

"What's gonna happen there? Is Erica gonna get him back?"

"There's no way that will happen," Diane explains. "We can't even find Erica. She still has outstanding warrants for her arrest. Even if she didn't, there would be things she would need to do to regain custody of him, starting with visiting regularly and completing a substance abuse assessment at least. She hasn't seen him since the night he came into care. Have you heard from her? Do you know where she is?"

"I ain't heard from that girl in months. I don't know where she's at."

Diane is looking at Gloria, but then her eyes move to me. I reach out for her hand again, so she reaches back. I love that. They keep talking, so I play with Diane's fingers until I pull them to my mouth and open wide.

"Little guy, you do not want to eat my fingers. They won't taste good." She pulls them away and tickles my belly just a little bit. I give her a big smile. She smiles back.

"You're adorable." She's talking to me now. I know she is. Suddenly, Alex hops up onto the couch and plops her head on my foot. Diane reaches out to pet her.

"Hey, is this your little buddy? You must like this little guy. I heard that scary growl before, but you can't fool me. You're sweet, too." Alex's ears perk up and she licks Diane's hand.

"Goodness, what's with you two and all the tongues?" She is smiling and so am I.

They all keep talking, but I stop listening. I'm too busy with Diane's fingers. And her hands. I'm trying to figure them out. There's no sizzle beneath the surface, like Gloria's. They aren't bony and cold like Wrinkles'. They are here and they are busy, paying attention to me and making me wish I could play with them some more.

At some point, they all stand up and I can tell Dawn and Diane are getting ready to leave.

"Oh, one more thing. I need to see where Buddy sleeps," Diane says to Gloria.

"What? Why do you need to do that?" Gloria asks.

"The court requires me to. It's a rule. I don't make the rules, but I do have to follow them. Can you show me?"

"His room is a mess," Gloria says.

"I don't mind. I have kids, too. I know how messy rooms can get. I just need to see it, and then I can get out of your way and you can get on with your day." Diane smiles. Gloria does not smile. Dawn does nothing.

"You can see it next time you come," Gloria says. "Not today."

"Is there a reason you don't want me to see where he sleeps?" Diane asks.

"Matter of fact, there is. You already taken up my whole morning. I got things to do and you got no business walking through my house. Caseworker done did that one time already before and that's good enough. Here I am, taking care of this baby and you got no respect for me. I'm tired of all this."

Gloria's mad. I can tell by the sound of her voice and the feel of her hands as she stands with me in her arms.

"So you're not going to let me see where he sleeps?"

"I just told you no."

"Okay. Well, it does concern me that you don't want to let me do a quick walk through."

Gloria does not respond. Dawn still does nothing. Alex looks from one to the other.

"It's my house. I can do as I please."

"I'll put in another referral for the developmental assessment," Dawn says, interrupting the words between Diane and Gloria.

"And I'll be in touch soon as well. Thanks for your time," Diane says. "Bye, little guy. See you soon."

As soon as they are out of sight, Gloria yells for Tony. "Come get this baby!"

Tony appears and takes me from Gloria's arms.

"They gone yet?" a voice yells from the bedroom.

It's Johnny. Johnny has been staying here for a little while. Sometimes he and Gloria are all tangled up in each other in the bedroom or on the couch and make wild noises. I don't know what they are doing, but I think they both like it.

"Yeah, they gone," Gloria yells back.

Tony puts me on the floor and walks away. Gloria disappears, too. The wild noises start again.

Alex lies next to me on the floor. I might as well go back to sleep.

CHAPTER 10

EVER SINCE JOHNNY GOT HERE, I haven't seen Squid. I don't know where he went.

I'm used to lots of people coming in and out of the house. Gloria and Johnny are used to it, too. In fact, they seem to like it when people come. They all pass things back and forth, things like money and other stuff. Nobody's mad so I don't know why Gloria gets mad when people come to see me.

I don't like the people who come and go. I have the same feeling I do when Gloria is holding me and I feel the sizzle in her hands. I feel like I'm teetering on the edge of disaster. So far, I've avoided it.

Alex and I try to stay clear of them as much as we can. We've been playing a new game. Alex started it. She brings me something like a shoe or a rag or a sock and drops it on the floor near me. As soon as I pick it up, she tries to grab it back with her mouth. We pull it back and forth until she lets it go, which she always does. Then I give it back to her and we start the whole thing over again. Even though Alex puts these things in her mouth, I don't, because I don't like the smell.

We play our games so much that my arms and hands can do things now they couldn't do before, like push off the floor when I'm on my belly. I can get around faster and faster now, too, like the little brown things that scurry across the floor and sometimes up the walls.

I'm starting to make more noise now that I'm doing more things with Alex. Sometimes I squeal when Alex and I play, but I stop when Johnny or Gloria yells at me. They don't like it when I make noise. It doesn't matter what kind.

I'm sitting on the floor when Alex brings a sock to me and drops it on my leg. Her ears are up high and she's waiting to play. I'm always up for playing with Alex, so I pick up the sock and she grabs the other end with her teeth. I squeal loudly as we each tug until she suddenly lets go. I wasn't ready, and I tumble over to the side. My ear and cheek hit the floor with a thud. I cry.

"Shut up!" Johnny yells from another room. I didn't mean to start crying. I almost never cry because first, nothing good happens when I do, and second, it's much better to try and stay quiet and out of the way.

This time, I can't help it. My ear has been hurting a lot. I used to pull on it because it felt funny but now it just hurts all the time. When I banged it on the floor, it was the worst thing I ever felt.

Alex tries to help by licking my ear, but it doesn't do any good, so she lies down beside me with her head close to mine. Sometimes Wrinkles comes when I cry, but she spends almost all her time in bed now.

I cry for a long time, but all that happens is Johnny yells louder and louder. It doesn't matter. I just can't stop. I try, but I can't.

Something Next is coming. I can feel it.

Johnny storms into the room. I was right. Something Next is here.

With a jerk, he picks me up by my leg. I remember this. My mom used to do this when I lived with her. The only difference is Johnny squeezes my leg so hard I think it might pop off.

The fur on Alex's back raises and she jumps up and starts barking. Johnny yells at her, too. She doesn't even care. She barks louder and louder and grabs his pants leg with her teeth. She must be mad because she would never try and play our tugging game with Johnny. I know that for sure.

"Shut up, you damn dog," Johnny roars as he kicks Alex and she goes flying across the room. She slams against the wall and lands in a heap on the floor.

I cry louder. Johnny swings me by the leg and hurls me across the room, too. My head hits the wall.

Everything goes dark.

When I open my eyes, Wrinkles is holding me with her bony hands. All of my body hurts and the ache in my ear is worse than ever. Stuff usually doesn't hurt like this, not even all the times I banged my head on things and the times hands hurt me.

This is different. I do my best to use my disappearing trick.

I think Alex hurts, too. She sleeps beside the chair where Wrinkles and I are sitting. I look around the room and I don't see Johnny or Gloria or Tony or anyone else. It is very quiet.

Wrinkles reaches for a bottle and puts it in my mouth. I didn't know I was hungry, but I gulp it down as fast as I can and just as quickly, it comes right back up. Alex's head immediately lifts off the floor and she quickly stands and lays her head across my foot in Wrinkles' lap. For as badly as I feel, I'm glad Alex is here with me. I reach out and put my hand on her head. She looks up at me with her big brown eyes. I know she won't ever hurt me. I know she will try to keep me safe even if it hurts her.

For now, that's all that matters.

I don't know how many days have passed since I hit the wall. All I know is everything has changed except for the ache in my ear. There's a new darkness in the house. It hangs in the air even when Johnny and Gloria are gone. I can't see it, but I can feel it in every nook and cranny of my body, both inside and outside. My skin stands on edge, like Alex's fur does sometimes when she gets angry or upset. I can feel it when I breathe, too. The air gets sucked into a giant, empty hole in my stomach, so sometimes I just take small little breaths while my heart pounds.

Alex and I both sleep more and more, but I always wake up fast when I hear Johnny's footsteps. I can tell which sounds belong to him and I try to brace myself in case his hands come for me. When they do, it always hurts.

I'm not the only one Johnny hurts. When he and Gloria yell at each other, he hurts her, too. This only makes things worse for me in two ways. First, I tense up even more and I feel stuck inside my body, wishing I could run away or disappear forever. My heart thumps against my chest so hard it hurts. Second, when Johnny hurts Gloria, she usually passes that hurt along to me. The sizzle in her hands has exploded. I can never avoid disaster anymore. I live in it full time. So does Alex.

My visitors have come to see me, but when they knock, no one answers the door. One time, Dawn came and she knocked and knocked and knocked. Finally, Tony picked me up and took me to another room and shut the door. I heard him pull the front door open with only one creak.

"Hi, Tony," Dawn said. "I don't know if you remember me, but I'm the Children's Services caseworker for Buddy. Is your mom home?"

"She ain't here," Tony said.

"Is Buddy here? I'd like to see him if he is."

"No, he's out with my mom. Nobody's home but me."

"Well, here's my card with my phone number. Can you please give it to her and let her know I've been trying to reach her?"

"Yes, ma'am," Tony said.

"Thank you, and thanks for answering the door. I thought I saw someone inside and I didn't want to leave until I was sure no one was here."

Then the door shut and the quiet returned. Tony never came back for me, which was just fine. Alex was curled up next to me on the floor. With her warm body next to mine and my hand holding her ear, we drifted off to sleep together.

Alex never barks much, but she does bark when the mailman comes. He is standing at the door and hands Gloria an envelope. She signs a piece of paper, hands it to him, shuts the door and rips the envelope open.

"What's that all about?" Johnny growls. His voice is always gruff.

"It's a letter from Children's Services. About Erica and Buddy. Looks like there's a copy of court papers in here, too."

"What do they want now?" he asks.

"Caseworker says here that she's been trying to reach me. She wants to know if I want custody of Buddy and it says I need to call her."

"Who's Erica?" Johnny asks.

"My cousin. Buddy's mama. She begged me to take him. So did my mama. Blood stays together."

"You want him?"

"I want Erica to come get him. He's her baby. She needs to take him. I done raised my kids. Tony's almost grown."

"If she ain't come around yet, she ain't going to. What are you gonna do if she don't?"

"I guess I have to keep him," Gloria says.

"Why don't you just give him back?"

"Give him back? To who? Foster care? Ain't happenin'."

"Why not? He ain't your problem."

"Maybe not, but I sure as hell ain't givin' him to those people. He don't belong to them. He belongs to us. Simple as that."

I don't know where I belong. I don't know who I have, except Alex, but I don't think I belong to her for real because for one thing, she has paws and I have hands. Neither of us uses words.

My eyes are heavy again. If I don't belong here, at least I can use my disappearing trick and go to sleep.

CHAPTER 11

I'VE BEEN LEARNING SINCE I got here. I don't mean to Gloria's—I mean since all the way back to when I lived with my mom. Maybe I don't talk and maybe I don't walk, but why would I? Who would listen to me anyway, and where would I go?

Even if I can't talk or walk, there's a lot of stuff I know. I know the world is a scary place where I never can be sure what will happen next. I know I have to take care of myself because no one else will. I know I don't matter very much because no one here seems to even see me, except when they are mad. I know there are more bad hands than good ones.

I only know one good thing, and that is Alex. I have learned things from her, too.

She taught me how to play. She taught me that I'm not alone, even though I'm scared sometimes. I know how nice it feels when she cuddles up next to me. Sometimes she makes me laugh.

She can't talk or feed me or fix my aching ear, even though I wish she could. I bet if she could, she would, and she would do a good job. She just doesn't have hands.

But she's *here* and somehow, that is enough. Knowing she loves me, even if she can't take care of me, is the only good thing I know.

Gloria is stirring a pot in the kitchen while Johnny stands by with a bottle in his hand. It's not the same as my bottle, but he puts his lips up to it and sucks it down. Maybe it's a big-person bottle.

"I been thinking. Tony 'bout to be fourteen and he wants to have some friends over for a party. I think that'd be alright with me," Gloria says.

"Don't make no difference to me. Better keep it small. We got a good thing going on here and we don't need no one bustin' it up. If there's a bunch of people here, it's gonna draw attention. We got to lay low." Johnny lets out a loud burp. Maybe the bottle makes that happen.

"We're just talking a couple kids. No big deal."

"As long as none of *your* people show up, 'cuz there's gonna be trouble if they do."

"You mean Squid and them? You all still up in each other's business? Let it go." Gloria is talking to Johnny. She's not looking at him though. She's looking at the pot on the stove.

"We got unfinished business and you know it. He owes me, and he better not show his face til he pays up."

"He says he don't owe you."

"He wrong. He owe me and he gonna pay, one way or the other." Johnny burps again.

"Well, I ain't seen him in weeks and I don't know where he is. Don't matter anyway. We're talking about a party with a couple teens, not Squid." Johnny walks over to Gloria and bends his head down toward the pot. "What's cookin'? Smells good."

For once, Johnny is right. It does smell good. My belly rumbles.

"Pantry got some hams and I was there at the right time. Threw some beans in, too." Gloria fishes a pile of food from the big pot and puts it on a plate. It sits on the counter and I watch it. My belly rumbles some more.

Johnny reaches for the plate and Gloria fills another one. Maybe this one is for me. I'm not sure it will be, but I hope so.

Tony walks in, grabs the plate off the counter, and walks back out without a word. Gloria puts more on another plate. Maybe this will be the one.

It's not. Gloria picks it up off the counter and begins to eat. She shovels the food into her mouth with one hand and gives a bottle to me with the other before she walks away.

A while later, the heat and smells in the kitchen begin to disappear.

Wrinkles arrives and stirs the pot before she moves it to the kitchen table.

"Cold. Not much here anyway," she says after she sticks her finger in it. She puts a little on a plate and then she's gone.

I chew on the top of my bottle for a while before I throw it across the room. Alex's ears perk up and she looks at me with her big brown eyes. Then she stands and stretches her short legs and hops onto a chair, and then onto the table. Her whole head disappears into the pot and when it comes out, she has a big bone in her mouth. She hops down and puts it on the floor in front of me. It smells amazing!

I pick it up with my hands and chew on it. Little bits of meat fall off into my mouth and it's the best thing I ever tasted. I knew these things popping through my gums were meant to do something. This must be it! I hold one hand out to Alex and she licks my fingers. I give her my other hand when she's done. The bone goes back and forth between my hands until there's nothing left for either of us.

I don't know when my belly ever felt this good.

CHAPTER 12

I WAKE UP TO THE SOUND of yelling.

"DAMNIT, MY FOOT!! What the hell did I just step on?" Tony is hopping on one foot while holding his other.

"What's all your hollering about?" Gloria yells from the other room.

"I stepped on a bone and it *hurt*." He picks up the bone and it flies across the room.

"I told you to clean up the kitchen last night. You old enough to have a party with a couple friends, you old enough to clean the house before they get here."

The screaming continues.

I wait for hands to come, knowing that if they do, they will have sizzle. I know it. I take short little breaths. I bet if I had fur like Alex, it would be standing up.

Enough time passes and I think the sizzle has, too. When someone finally comes for me, it's Wrinkles, and her hands never sizzle. Whew!

There's a party going on here. At least, that's what I think it is. People are stuffed into the house, some kneeling on the floor around tables and some piled onto the couch. Some are even piled on top of each other in the chair where Wrinkles used to sit all time. The air is hazy with smoke.

Music is blaring and, as usual, my ear is throbbing. It has been hurting for so long now I can hardly remember when it didn't. I've kind of gotten used to it. I don't have any choice. When it gets real bad, I use my disappearing trick on it. I pretend it has gone away, just like I can pretend to disappear when I need to.

I am passed from person to person. I'm in the arms of some woman when I hear a voice I've heard before.

"Hey, little Buddy, how you been?" It's Squid, the man, the one who used to talk to me. He hasn't been here for a while. He takes me in his arms.

Because I'm mostly disappeared all the time now, I don't smile back or even move.

The woman hands me off to him and he balances me in one arm while he uses his other hand to smoke.

Out of the corner of my eye, I see Johnny. His eyes are fixated on me and White T-Shirt. I don't know why, but I know it's not a good thing. I take little breaths. I wonder if they can see my heart pounding.

Johnny is walking toward us. He comes face-to-face with Squid but doesn't say a word. I wait.

Something Next is coming. I can feel it.

"How you been?" Squid asks as he extends a hand out to Johnny. Somehow, Squid is able to talk with a small smoky thing sitting between his lips. Maybe it's one of his tricks.

Johnny's fist brushes against the top of my head and then hits Squid's jaw with such force that he stumbles. He loses his grip, and I fall to the ground and land on top of Alex. It hurts, but not as much as it could have.

All I can see from where I land is feet. They are everywhere, just like the loud and ugly shouts that have drowned out the music. Hands scoop me off the floor then I move to other hands. Maybe they are Gloria's. Maybe Johnny's. Maybe they are hands I've never felt before. Maybe it doesn't even matter, because all of them are terrifying.

I see Alex trying to reach me, but there are too many legs and feet between us. Two loud popping noises shatter my ears, and then the screaming starts. It's not my screaming, though. I don't make a sound as my body hurls through the air.

Maybe I disappeared forever.

CHAPTER 13

"HE WAS UNCONSCIOUS BUT BREATHING on his own when he arrived via squad yesterday in the early morning hours."

The words are light and airy, just like my whole body. They float around the room like I do and there is nothing but total peace. Not even my ear hurts anymore.

Thank goodness.

I lift my eyelids a few times before they actually open.

"Well, look who's coming back to us. Hello, Michael. We've been waiting for you."

Maybe this voice is talking to me, but I don't know. Who's Michael? I have no idea. My name is Buddy.

I blink my eyes some more and look up at the man with the voice. He's in a white coat and I think I've been here before, but maybe not. This isn't Gloria's house. I know that for sure. For one thing, it is bright here and at Gloria's, it is always dark. The sounds and smells are all different, too.

There's not just one man in a white coat, either. There are more, and some are men and some are women. Then there are some that don't wear white coats. I've never seen any of these faces before. I'm sure of it.

It's another Something Next. I'm too tired to see what it is. My eyelids drop again.

The light and airy feeling leaves my body and suddenly everything is heavy and everything hurts. My head. My belly. My arms and legs. And what's worse, I am trapped. I'm surrounded by metal bars, and there are big things on one of my legs and one of my arms. I couldn't move them even if I wanted to. I'm buried under the weight of it all. Besides, there's something in my other arm hooked up to a line that ends at a machine near my bed. I don't know what it is, but I don't think I like it.

I look from one side to the other and I don't see Alex anywhere. I don't know where I am or where she went, but she must be here somewhere. She always stays with me.

I try and try and try to flip over onto my belly. Maybe if I do that, I will see her.

It's useless. The heavy things won't let me. There's an ache in my chest that feels as bad as the ache in my bones, but it's a different kind of hurt. It's empty and awful and scary, but I don't cry. I just want Alex.

I don't know what to do, so I move my head back and forth, back and forth, *swish swish*, and suddenly the room gets brighter. Did my head do that? I don't know how. There are people walking into my room. Did one of them make the room brighter? Maybe. There's a whole line of them. They stand on both sides of my crib.

"This is Michael Wilson, eighteen months old. He presents with fractures to the fifth and sixth right ribs; left ribs six through ten. Fracture to right humerus and right femur. Patient also has a subdural hematoma and skull fracture. CT scan showed no brain bleed, although we'll need to keep a close eye on him to make sure it stays that way. The most astonishing news, however, is that we extracted a cockroach from his right ear."

There's a knock on the door. All the heads turn to look.

It's Wrinkles. She has a man with her, but I don't know him.

"Hello, ma'am. Are you family?" asks the White Coat who does all the talking.

"Yes, I'm the great aunt. This is Pastor Hartman from my church. He brought me here."

"Are you the one who came in with Michael initially?"

"What do you mean?" Wrinkles looks confused.

"When he came in, he was accompanied by a relative who left

shortly after arrival. We haven't seen any family since."

"Yes, sir, that was me. I didn't want the baby to go all by himself, but it was awful late. So once I saw he was in good hands, I left."

"There's been a lot of confusion about who's been caring for him and what happened that got him to this point. Are you his guardian?"

"No, sir, not me. He's my sister's baby's baby. His mama is on drugs real bad and Children's Services took him away. He was in foster care then he came to live with my daughter, Gloria. I live with her, too," Wrinkles explains.

"Can you tell us what happened that brought him into the emergency room?"

"No, sir, I really can't. I don't know."

"But you were there, right? You came in with him."

"I sure did come in with him, but I don't know what happened. I'm gettin' old and my mind don't always follow. Know what I mean? All I know is, there were some people who stopped by to visit and next thing I know, there's sirens and police cars and Buddy being taken away on a stretcher. That's all I can tell you. He gonna be alright?"

Wrinkles is old. And sad. And very tired, and she doesn't have an Alex to make her feel better, like I do. Suddenly, I feel sad for her.

Talking White Coat is not old or sad or tired. He has a look on his face that seems angry, but not the sizzle kind of angry.

"Michael ... or is Buddy his nickname?"

"Everybody call him Buddy. When you first said Michael, I didn't know who you was talking about."

"Buddy has experienced pretty significant trauma. He has multiple injuries. Some tests we ran showed he has old fractures as well that happened before this latest incident."

"I don't know how any of that could have happened," Wrinkles says. "Gloria take real good care of Buddy. His bones gonna heal, right?"

"They will. He also suffered a skull fracture and a subdural hematoma, which means there's been bleeding between his brain and the skull. We'll need to watch him carefully for a couple of days, but so far, there hasn't been any sign of bleeding inside his brain, which is good news. He had to take quite a hard hit to have these kinds of injuries, though. Probably multiple hard hits."

The air in the room is tense and sad and angry all at the same time, and it's coming from all directions, as far as I can tell. I don't know if the others can feel it, but I can, just as much as I can feel these heavy things on my arm and leg.

"How long he gonna be here? When's he comin' home?" Wrinkles asks.

"That's something for Children's Services and the court to decide. But given his injuries ..."

It's quiet for a minute, and Talking White Coat opens his mouth then closes it again. I think he's going to say more, but he doesn't.

"I don't understand." Wrinkles is crying. "You mean you think *we* did this to him? You think we hurt him on purpose? We'd never do that. We love Buddy. He flesh and blood."

"Right now, there are a lot of questions to be answered and things to be sorted out. I'm sure the caseworker and detective assigned to his case will be in contact with you all soon, if they haven't been already."

"Detective?" Wrinkles is crying harder. The man beside her puts his arm around her, but he doesn't say anything.

"Like I said, they'll be in touch. In the meantime, we need to talk with Gloria or whoever can give us some important background information. We have to know as much as possible about Buddy and his past care and physical health in order to give him the best medical care we can. Do you think you could help us with that piece? Can you get Gloria in here to speak to us?"

"Yes, of course she'll come. She been worried sick about Buddy."

Talking White Coat has a funny look on his face. He opens his mouth to say something, but he doesn't. Instead, he just closes it again. Maybe it's one of his tricks.

It's quiet until the silence is broken by the shuffle of dozens of shoes moving across the floor.

I don't know if Something Next is coming, and I don't really care.

"Hey, little Buddy, look who's awake. It took you long enough."

I've heard this voice off and on since I've been here. This is the first time I hear it when my eyes are open, though, and now I see the face that goes with the voice. It's new.

The hands move gently across my body. They are soft. I like them.

"You've had quite a go of it. You really needed your rest, but I'm glad to see your pretty brown eyes open." Soft Hands smiles at me.

Soon after, more people come into the room. They are all in white coats. Maybe they live in white coats.

I watch them carefully while one of them does things like flash lights in my eyes. They all talk to each other, but they don't talk to me. After a while, they all disappear except for Soft Hands.

"Well, Buddy, it looks like you could use a little cleaning up. Why don't we get that going?" Soft Hands walks around the room and gathers things together before she returns to my crib.

Her voice continues as her hands run warm soapy water all over my body. She's extra careful in all the hurt places. I've never had such gentle hands take care of me like this. Soft Hands is talking to me, too, and I love that *of course*. Somehow, it makes all the hurt not as bad.

The heavy things on my leg and arm are still weighing me down and I still feel trapped. I guess it could be worse. At least my ear feels a million times better.

Once I sit up to eat, I get my first look around the room. Alex has to be here somewhere. I turn my head all around, as much as I can.

Where could she be? She's always right here.

"Come on, Buddy. You need to eat." Soft Hands has been waving a spoon with squishy stuff around in front of my face. I don't want it.

After a while, Soft Hands gives up. She gently puts me back in my crib. I look around one more time for Alex.

When I still don't see her, I roll my head back and forth, back and forth, *swish swish* until all is dark and quiet.

CHAPTER 14

"YOU WEREN'T SUPPOSED TO COME back like this." A quiet voice whispers as a hand strokes the top of my head.

This hand feels so nice. Have I felt this one before? I'm not sure. Maybe I'm dreaming, because I think I'm still asleep. At least a little bit asleep.

She keeps talking. I love that, *of course*!

"I thought about you every day after you left the hospital the last time. I always wanted to see you again, but I never wanted it to be like this."

My sleepy eyes are open now and my visitor lowers the railing of my crib, kisses me on my forehead, and touches my nose with the tip of her finger. Have I seen her before?

"Can I sit with you a little bit?" I don't answer because I don't use words. I would say yes if I could.

She scoops up all of me, even my heavy leg and heavy arm, and all the cords to the machines don't even get in the way. She must have done this before. Maybe it's one of her tricks.

She lowers us into a rocking chair and for a long time, we rock back and forth, back and forth, but my head doesn't go *swish swish*. Instead, it rests against her chest where I can hear the slightest *thump thump*. I do know these hands. I know this *thump thump*. I'm sure of it.

"Hey, Maggie, you know this little guy?" Soft Hands is standing in the doorway.

"Yeah, I do. He came through the ER months ago, after being abandoned in a car. I stayed with him while the caseworker was waiting on a foster home. It took hours."

"Did he go to a foster home when he left here? Because when he was brought in this time, he had been living with a relative."

"Yeah, he went to a foster home. I guess he went to a relative afterwards. I told the caseworker I wished I could take him home with me that first night, but of course, I wasn't allowed."

"Really? I love kids, but I've never wanted to take one home with me."

"I hadn't either, until then. If I'd taken him home that night, he wouldn't be here right now. None of this would have happened." Maggie sounds sad. I can feel it. I feel sad, too.

It's a long time before any more words are said and I am glad. I just want to rock back and forth and listen to her *thump thump*. After a long magic time, Maggie puts me back into my crib, but I don't want to go. I want to stay with her and her *thump thump*. For the first time since I've been here, I start to cry. I can't help it.

"Now now, little Buddy, it's going to be okay. I'll come and see you again later. I promise. Oh, I almost forgot. I brought you a little present."

She holds out something furry. It's white and brown with four legs.

ALEX! I wish I knew how to say Alex in words, but I don't even though I try.

"I figured this little dog could keep you company. He's awful cute, and I thought you'd like him. Looks like I was right!"

I know it's not my Alex, because for one, the paws don't move and it doesn't lick me. And it's not as big as my Alex. But somehow, it feels a little bit like Alex anyway. I make more noise.

"So you *do* like him. Maybe we should name him. What's a good name for a furry friend like this?"

I make some more sounds, but none of them are words.

"Did you say X? Kind of sounds like it." I make some more noise.

"So you think we should name him X?" I make some more noise again.

"That's an interesting choice for a dog's name, but if you say so, X it is. Hey, look at this." She brings the stuffed animal closer so I can see it better.

"See this little patch of white fur? I think it kind of looks like an X. Maybe I'm going crazy. You'd think I was the one who took a hit to the head."

She laughs, and it's the first time I've heard a laugh in a long, long time. I miss that sound. I love that I get to hear it now. I almost smile.

But not quite.

CHAPTER 15

HALF ASLEEP AND HALF AWAKE, I hear a quiet swish of shoes crossing the floor. The sound stops when there's a knock on the door. Someone pushes it open.

"I'm Dawn from Children's Services."

Ah-ha! I know this voice. This lady came to see me at Gloria's house.

"I'm his nurse today. My name is Paula," says the lady with the shoes that swished.

"How's he doing?" Dawn takes a few steps forward.

"Alright. Still sleeping quite a bit. We're keeping a close eye on him."

I flutter my eyes and decide to open them. Right away, I see my new Alex. I reach out to grab him and rub his fur on my face.

"Look who's awake! Hi, sleepy guy. You have a visitor." I like Paula's voice.

Dawn looks down at me in my crib and doesn't say a word. There's water in her eyes and it spills onto her cheeks. She turns away.

"Sounds like things got a little crazy in that house that night," Paula says.

"I can't comment on that," Dawn replies.

"I guess you don't really have to. I saw it on the news. Shots fired. At least Buddy dodged the bullets. That's something in his favor, I guess."

"I've been talking with the hospital social worker, and she's been giving me updates. I just came by because I wanted to lay eyes on him myself." Dawn is talking to Paula. She is not talking to me. Dawn is my visitor. Why won't she talk to me?

"Where will he go when he leaves here?" Paula asks.

"Probably to a foster home."

"Do you have one in mind?"

"No, and we won't really start looking for one until we have a discharge date."

No more words are spoken, not even to me. Paula's hands run over my body, stopping in certain places then fidgeting with the machine by my bed.

There's another knock on the door. Both Paula and Dawn look up.

Maggie has come back to see me!

"Hey, Maggie, I heard you've been by to visit," Paula says.

"Yeah, just thought I'd pop in and see how the little guy is doing this morning." She walks toward me. My eyes follow every move. "So, how is he?" She reaches out for my hand and kisses it when I wrap my fingers around one of hers.

"I was just telling Dawn, he's still pretty groggy and sleeping a lot, which we'd expect, given what he's been through. Dawn is his Children's Services caseworker."

Maggie turns toward Dawn.

"Oh, hi," she says. "I'm Maggie. I work in the ER. It's nice to meet you. So, you're Buddy's caseworker?"

"Yes. Do you know him?"

"I do. I was his nurse when he came through the ER a few months ago. We spent a lot of time together while you guys were looking for a foster home. When he left the ER, he was going to a foster home, but I guess he didn't stay there."

"No, he didn't."

"Well, I'm glad to meet you. I was going to try and find out the contact information for his caseworker."

"Oh, really?" Dawn asks. She looks confused.

"Yes. I wanted to inquire about the possibility of Buddy being placed with me. My husband and I recently became certified foster parents. We finished our classes last month and all of our paperwork was done and submitted. We literally just got licensed last week and are waiting for a placement."

"You're a foster parent?" Dawn looks surprised.

"Yep! It's something we always talked about doing, but we planned to wait a few years. When it took hours and hours for the other caseworker to find a home for Buddy the first time, I realized there were kids who needed homes today—not years from now. So, we looked into it, and yes, we just got certified." Maggie has a smile on her face. I can hear it in her voice, too.

"You became a foster parent for Buddy?" Dawn looks confused again. She looks this way a lot.

"No, not for Buddy. I didn't think I'd ever see Buddy again. We became foster parents because there are kids who need homes now. So, my question is, since I'm licensed, what can I do to have Buddy placed in my home?"

"Well, it doesn't really work like that. Once we have a discharge date, I'll make a referral for a foster home and we'll see what comes up."

"What comes up? I'm already up!" Maggie says. She's smiling again. I love when she smiles. It makes me want to smile.

"Unless you are a relative or have had the child in your home previously, you would be considered the same as every other foster family that meets the criteria for a toddler."

"That doesn't seem to make a lot of sense," Paula says. Now she looks confused. "If Maggie's a licensed foster parent and a nurse and knows Buddy, why not place him in her home?"

"I don't have any control over where he's placed," Dawn replies.

"But aren't you his caseworker? If you don't have control over where he's placed, who does?" Now they all look confused.

"I make a referral for a foster home, someone from my agency finds one, and then I get the name and number. That's the process."

Maggie shakes her head. "I'm totally confused. If he needs a placement and I'm approved and I know him, why wouldn't you place him with me?"

"I already told you. We have a process. We can't circumvent the process."

"*Circumvent the process?* Isn't the process made for children, and not the other way around?" Paula asks.

"We can't back-door placements. Maggie, you can't jump to the head of the line just because you were his nurse a few months ago. It isn't fair to families who've been waiting for a toddler."

"Shouldn't this be about what's fair to Buddy? Besides, last time he needed a home, there wasn't exactly a line of foster parents wanting to take him. I see billboards and ads calling for foster parents all the time. There was an article in the paper just the other day about the critical shortage of foster homes and how the community needs to step up and take care of these kids. This is me stepping up. Let me step up for Buddy." Maggie's voice is just a tiny bit louder than it was before. She's not smiling anymore.

"We can't circumvent the process," Dawn says again. "Besides, it might not even matter. We still have to rule out other relatives."

"I thought you said he was probably going to go to a foster home," Paula says.

"I said probably. It's not definite."

There's silence again. I rub Alex's fur against my cheek.

Everything in the room feels different. It's not a good different. I'm not sure what it is, but it doesn't feel as good as before, and definitely not as good as when I lay my head on Maggie's chest and hear her *thump thump*.

I think it's another Something Next.

CHAPTER 16

I WAKE UP TO THE SOUND of crying, but it's not mine. First of all, I know when I'm crying, and it is not me. Second, this crying is so loud and so big, it is hurting my ears. I couldn't be that loud even if I wanted!

"I told you! I don't know nothin' 'bout what happened to my baby. Y'all took him from me and look at him now. He ain't never looked like this when he was with me. Never. I took good care of him."

I freeze. I know this voice. It's my *mom*.

I haven't heard her voice since the night in the car when we went fast, fast, fast and the lights and sirens chased us until she ran away. I haven't felt her hands, good or bad, since she put me in the back seat of that car on that cold, cold night and left me there.

"Mikey!" she yells. "You awake!"

Did she think I could sleep through all *that*? Now that my ear is all better, I can hear just fine.

"We didn't take him from you. You left him," Dawn says.

"Well, not anymore. I want him back. He's my son."

"Ms. Wilson, you've got charges and a trial pending. Resisting arrest. Disorderly conduct. Drug possession. Child endangerment. You're looking at jail time. They might have turned you out after they picked you up, but you are far from free and clear." This time, a man is speaking. He's not wearing a white coat, though. I've never seen him before.

"Listen, mister. I don't care if you a detective or not. You got nothing to do with my court case. We talkin' about Mikey." My mom is mad.

"Erica, Detective Bates is here from the Office of Personal Crimes.

He has a lot to do with everything related to your son, including your current criminal case." Now Dawn is talking. She turns to the man. "How is it that you guys picked her up, processed her, and we didn't even know it? As far as I knew, she was still on the run."

"Breakdown in communication, I guess."

"I don't need to sit here and take all this. What matters is my boy's all broken up and all you wanna do is talk about me. Well, I ain't got nothing to say to you." My mom stands up real fast. Her chair falls over and makes a loud crash on the floor. She leans over, kisses me on the forehead, and just like that, she is gone. Again.

Dawn and the detective look at each other.

"Well, that's par for the course," Detective says. "No one has anything to say about what happened that night at the house. A house full of people, and not one will talk."

"Do you think she was there?" Dawn asks.

"No, I don't think so. We do know there's been a lot going on in that house for months. Police have been monitoring it for quite some time. Suspected drug activity. It was only a matter of time until they upended the whole operation."

"And no one bothered to tell us that, either?"

"I guess not. Maybe they didn't know you all were involved. They might not have even known a kid was living there, if he never left the house."

There's a long pause and they both look at me. I don't know why they are here or what they want. Suddenly, I want Alex, my *real* Alex. I look around the room one more time, thinking maybe she is finally here now. Instead, I see my new Alex, the one that doesn't move or make any noise. I grab her and rub her ear between the finger and thumb on my good hand.

"Where did that stuffed animal come from?" the man asks.

"I have no idea," Dawn says. "Strangely, it looks a little bit like the dog that lived in that house. Let me tell you, that dog was glued to Buddy's side. Every time I made a visit, I didn't see one without the other."

"That must have been the dog that was injured at the house that night."

"What happened to it?" There's a new energy in Dawn's voice that I've never heard before.

"Took a bullet. In the leg. As far as I know, she's doing alright. One of the officers on the scene has a soft spot for animals. She's always taking them in. She has a brother who's a vet and she took it straight to his office. That dog is in good hands."

"That's good news. Well, at least the dog is safe now."

They are both looking at me again. They don't say anything, but I can tell they are thinking. I can see it in their faces.

"So what's your plan for Buddy?"

"Probably foster care, at least until things get sorted out. There's another relative who might pan out, but it'll take a while to get all the background checks and paperwork done. Of course, there's a chance Mom could go to drug treatment instead of jail, and if that's the case, we'd look at visits and reunification with her. It's really up in the air," Dawn says.

"Sounds like maybe that dog was the lucky one."

"Maybe. Probably." Dawn sighs. Her sigh hangs heavy, almost as heavy as the things on my leg and arm.

"Are you charging anyone in relation to the injuries Buddy sustained?"

"Not yet." This time he sighs heavily. "You know how these things go. If we can't pinpoint exactly who hurt him, then we can't charge anyone. There have been so many people in and out of that house, I can't guarantee we'll ever know."

Their heavy sighs cover me like a big, heavy blanket. There are no smiles. No laughing. No kisses on my head or fingers touching the tip of my nose.

At least my ear doesn't hurt anymore. That was the worst. My belly doesn't ache either, and I have my new Alex to rub against my cheek. Sometimes, I hold her paws between my fingers and move them back and forth, and that feels good—but not as good as my real Alex.

78

"Dawn, it's been nice to meet you. I'm heading out. Due in court just after lunch." He hands her a card. "I'll be in touch."

Dawn reaches in a big bag with all her papers and pulls out a card the same size. I don't know how she found it in that big thing. Maybe it's one of her tricks.

"Great. I'm heading out too, so I'll walk with you."

Neither one says goodbye. They never talked to me or touched me the whole time they were here.

I rub my fingers back and forth on my new Alex's paw and wait for Maggie to come.

CHAPTER 17

I DON'T KNOW HOW MANY DAYS I've been here with all the white coats. I don't know why everyone else gets to come and go, but I don't ever get to leave. I'm not sure where I'd go anyway, so I guess it doesn't really matter. Maybe I will stay here forever.

"Hey, sweet little boy. How's my buddy today?"

I look up from my new Alex. Maggie is here. It's always my favorite part of the day. Sometimes she even comes twice. I know the sound of her footsteps, and sometimes I can hear them before I even see her. I listen very close for them now that my ear is all better.

Every time she comes to see me, she smiles and the room feels happy. She talks to me the whole time which I love, *of course*. More and more, I try to talk to her. Maybe one day I will say a real word that sounds like the words big people say. I'm not sure, though.

The best thing we do together is sit in a chair and rock back and forth, back and forth and I get to hear her *thump thump*.

She scoops me out of my crib and kisses me on my head. She always does that. She's the only one who ever has.

She is very quiet today as I lay my head on her chest and listen to her *thump thump*. For some reason, the room doesn't feel happy. I don't think about that, though. I just listen for her *thump thump*. It's the safest, most comfy place I've ever been. I feel as good as I used to feel when my real Alex laid beside me. Even better. Thinking about Alex makes me miss her even more than I usually do. I let out a big sigh. There is sad everywhere, even though I'm in my favorite place. I can feel it.

"I hope you know how much I love you," Maggie says. "I'd give anything to take you home with me and to love you forever and watch you grow big and strong. When you grow up, you'll be able to do or be anything you want. You are so smart."

There are no words for a long time. Just *thump thump*.

"I know your new foster family will love you. Even though you're going to live with someone else, I'll still love you forever. I'll be with you always, too, because you are in my heart and I'm in yours. I'll think about you and pray for you every day." A drop of water falls onto the top of my head. Maybe it came from her cheek. I don't know where it came from, but she wipes it away with her thumb.

"I guess this is what it means to literally cry over somebody," she says as she laughs, even though she's sad. I love that sound.

For a long, long time I sit and soak up her *thump thump* until it feels like it is a part of me. No one can take that away.

Nothing else matters right now, not even Something Next, whatever it is.

CHAPTER 18

THIS IS THE DAY I get to leave. At least, I think it is. I can feel it. There are lots of people in and out of the room. Some of them I know, like Paula, who takes care of me a lot. Some, I've never seen before. I look from one face to another and try to figure out what will happen next.

Dawn appears at the door but she doesn't knock. I think it's because all of her hands are full. She's carrying her big bag with all her papers and she has a car seat, too. It's not my car seat, I know that for sure, but it is definitely a car seat. I think it's for me.

"Here are his discharge instructions along with upcoming appointments. He's due in the orthopedic clinic in two weeks. He's also scheduled for a full developmental assessment next week." A White Coat gives Dawn some papers. She sets the car seat on the floor and reaches her hand out. She barely looks at the papers before stuffing them in her bag.

"Here's information on cast care. The casts are waterproof, but they take a long time to dry and that isn't ideal for a baby's skin, so I'd advise against it. He can continue with sponge baths for now." More papers disappear into Dawn's big bag.

"He should follow up with his pediatrician within three days. Will he be returning to the clinic where's he been seen before?" White Coat asks.

"I'm not really sure," Dawn says. "That's up to the foster parents." White Coat nods.

"That covers everything," White Coat says. "Do you have any questions?"

"I don't think so," Dawn says.

"When you're ready to go, Joe here can help you out."

"Sure thing." A man steps forward. "Let me give you a hand with all this stuff." He picks up the car seat and a bag that sits on the chair by my crib.

"Thanks," Dawn says. She picks me up carefully from my crib and holds me awkwardly in her arms. Suddenly, I'm afraid she's going to drop me. I want to cry, but I don't. I just want Maggie. She knows how to hold me and I'm never scared when I'm with her. I look around the room for my new Alex, but I don't see her, either. Now I start to cry. I can't help it. I want Maggie. I want my old Alex. I want my new Alex. I just want something I know.

Dawn carries me screaming down the hall while Joe follows with my stuff.

"Wait!"

Paula is running down the hall toward us, waving my new Alex in the air. "You can't leave without this." I reach out for it with my good hand. Paula rubs my head then puts her two hands on my cheeks. "We'll miss you, little Buddy."

Joe stands with me in his arms while we wait for Dawn and her car. When she pulls up, she gets out and disappears into the back with the car seat. She fights with it for a long time.

"Good enough," I hear her say as she tugs on the straps. Joe hands me over and Dawn sits me down. She puts my good arm under one strap but can't get the other arm under the other strap. She pulls and pulls but it is no use. She sighs and readjusts my body. I still don't fit right.

I'm not sure, but I think Dawn is trying not to cry. Her face is scrunched up and her eyes are watery. Her arms are rigid and although she isn't hurting me, I'm not sure that she won't. I stay very still and quiet.

"Let me see what I can do," Joe says as he steps forward. "Here, you hold him for a minute and let me work on these straps." Now Joe disappears into the car. When he emerges, he holds his hands out and Dawn passes me to him.

Much better. He buckles me in and I hold my new Alex up to my face and rub her fur back and forth, back and forth. The car begins to move and we drive for a long, long time. We drive for so long that I can't keep my eyes open anymore.

Another Something Next.

I hardly care.

CHAPTER 19

THE CAR COMES TO A stop and I rub my eye with the back of my good hand. I hear voices outside, and when I turn my head, there are two little smiling faces looking at me through the window. There's the bottom half of a bigger person, too.

Car doors open and close and Dawn reaches in to unbuckle me. She lifts me from the seat and we come face to face. I stare at her. Hers is the only face I've seen a lot of times, no matter where I live.

"Can I hold him?" Little arms are reaching up for me.

"Not yet," the bigger person says as she holds the hand on the end of one of the little arms. "Hi, I'm Maxine," she says to Dawn.

"Nice to meet you. This is Buddy," Dawn says. I don't move. Instead, I try to pull my disappearing act.

My body is tired and so am I. I'm tired of new faces and places. I'm tired of listening and watching and waiting to see if hands are bad or good or what they will do to me. I'm tired of never knowing what is going to happen. I'm just tired. Of everything.

"Hi Buddy," Maxine says. She holds out her arms and Dawn hands me over. I start screaming, even though it makes all my insides hurt. I don't even really mind the hurting. I'm used to something hurting mostly all the time.

Maxine carries me into a small house with the two little faces trailing behind along with Dawn and her big bag of papers.

I'm still screaming.

"He's not usually like this," Dawn explains. She looks confused a lot. Right now, she just looks like she has no idea what to do.

"Why don't you get his paperwork and things and I'll try to calm him," Maxine says. Dawn disappears out the front door.

"Mom, why's he crying so much? Doesn't he want to live with us?" One of the little faces is looking up at Maxine.

"Maybe he's crying because his arm and leg hurt," the other little face says.

"This little guy has been through a lot. He doesn't know us and he's probably scared. He'll settle down. Why don't you two go and play for a bit while I talk to his caseworker?"

The two disappear but return just as quickly.

"Here," says one as she holds up my new Alex. "His caseworker told me to give this to him. It's his favorite. Here Buddy, do you want your doggy?"

I am still screaming, even though my insides are killing me.

Dawn and Maxine go over all the papers that came with me, but they do it fast. The two people with little faces keep trying to give me stuff, but I don't want it. I wish I could use my disappearing trick on them! Finally, Maxine tells them to "Let him be," whatever that means.

After Dawn and the little faces are gone, Maxine sits me on her lap and gives me a bottle. My heavy arm and leg don't seem to bother her and they don't get in the way. I'm comfortable here. Maybe this will be alright. Or maybe I should start screaming again.

I think I'll start screaming again. So I do. I scream and scream and scream some more. The little faces pop into the doorway of the room and stare at me with big eyes.

"Mom, what is *wrong* with him?"

"There's nothing wrong with him. He's just letting off a little steam. You girls let off plenty in your baby days. Iris, you cried your whole first six months. Sometimes, I thought you'd never stop—but you're not screaming now, right?"

"Right."

"And Esme, don't tell me you don't know a thing or two about having a temper. When you're mad, you sure do have a way of letting people know. Am I right?"

"Right."

"So, we're just going to take our time. He'll get settled soon enough."

"I hope so. My ears hurt."

"Look, I think he's going to stop!"

It's true. My screams have turned to sniffles.

"Hi there, little Buddy. You don't have to cry. It's okay." I look from one little face to the other and then I start screaming again.

"On second thought, he is probably sore and hurting. I'm sure this is the most he's moved since he got to the hospital. His broken bones and ribs will take time to heal. Esme, can you get me his medicine? It's in the bag the worker left."

Even though I'm screaming and squirming, Maxine finds a way to shoot the thick, sweet stuff into the back of my mouth. Down it goes.

But I'm still screaming.

CHAPTER 20

THE FIRST THING I SEE when I wake up is my new Alex, who is sitting in the corner of my crib. I don't know where I am, but at least I have her with me. I reach out for her paw and hold her while I move my head back and forth and listen to the *swish swish*.

The door creaks open. Someone is coming. My heart starts pounding and I take little breaths. I don't know who it is or what kind of hands they have.

It's one of the little faces.

"Hi, Buddy. Did you have a good nap?" Her voice is quiet. She reaches in and pats me on my head.

My bottom is squishy, my arm and leg are heavy, and I'm a little sweaty, too.

"Mom! Buddy's awake!" Her loud voice startles me. I liked her better quiet.

"You didn't wake him, did you Esme?" Maxine asks.

"No, I promise. I heard him making noise and I came in and he was awake." Her voice is quiet again. Well, at least more quiet than it was.

Maxine's arms reach in for me. Her face is very close to mine and I don't know why or what she is going to do so I stay very still. She kisses me on the cheek.

That wasn't so bad.

"Can I change him?"

"You can help by getting me a diaper and wipes." Maxine lays me down and begins to take my pants off. "Oh boy, this is going to be harder than I thought."

Goopy brown stuff slides all over my behind and on the backs of my legs. My belly gurgles and more of that stuff falls out of me.

"Whoa, okay. Goodness, you're going to need a bath and I'm defi-nitely going to need a helper." Maxine wipes as much of the stuff off me as she can. "Esme, go start the water in the baby bathtub. Make sure it's not too hot or cold. Just right." Esme disappears.

"You didn't tell me he was awake!!" The other little face is now in mine. She's loud.

"It wasn't a secret, Iris. Can you grab me a couple of plastic bags?" Maxine begins unbuttoning my shirt and slides my good arm out of the sleeve and then my heavy arm. Except for my heavy things, I'm totally naked. A steady stream of wet flies through the air.

"Eww, he's peeing!" Why is Iris so loud? She scares me. I might start screaming again. I'm not sure yet.

"It's okay, Buddy. Don't cry. We'll get you all nice and clean." Maxine carries me into the bathroom and stops suddenly. "Oh, I forgot. He can't have a real bath. Girls, get me three of the big towels and lay them down here on the floor next to the tub."

Iris runs off and returns with towels in hand. She piles them on the floor and Maxine puts me on top of them.

This is the weirdest place I've ever been. I'm so surprised, I don't even start screaming.

The washing begins. Maxine starts with my head and works her way down, being extra careful with the heavy parts. By the time she is done, there is water everywhere. The little hands help me get dry. The big hands do my diaper and pull my heavy arm then good arm through the sleeves of a big soft shirt.

"I'm home!" It's a voice I haven't heard before.

"We're all upstairs. Be down in a minute." Footsteps get closer and closer. They belong to a boy. He is tall.

"Whoa, what happened here?" he says.

"Just a little explosion followed by a very tricky bath. Meet Buddy," Maxine says. "He's going to be here for a while."

"Cool. A dude. About time we had another boy around here. What's up with the girly t-shirt?"

"He came with just the clothes on his back, and those happen to

89

be covered in something we don't need to talk about. I'll run to the store tonight. How was school, Theo?"

"School was school. What's for dinner?"

"Your dad is going to pick up pizza on his way home. See if James' mom can take you to basketball. I don't want to have to drag Buddy back out tonight."

Maxine stands and puts me on her hip. I just kind of hang there. The little faces stand up, too.

"Okay," Theo says. He reaches for my hand. "Hey, Buddy. These two turkeys driving you crazy yet? Join the club."

"We are NOT turkeys!" I can't tell for sure if Iris and Esme are mad.

I'm not sure what to make of all this. I look from one face to another to another. Then I start screaming again, even though it makes my insides hurt.

CHAPTER 21

THIS IS MY VERY FIRST time sitting at a table with this many people. I'm feeling better now. Nothing hurts and with my good hand, I try to put small bits of food in my mouth, but I keep missing. It's annoying.

There are five faces at the table. One is Maxine. The kids call her "Mom." The two little faces are called Iris and Esme. Iris is bigger than Esme. The boy is called Theo.

There's a man at the table, too. The kids call him "Dad" but Maxine calls him "Will." When he came home, he brought two thin boxes with him and they smelled amazing.

"Remember the first time we got a foster baby, and people brought us dinner for like a week?" Theo asks.

"Oh yeah, and they always brought dessert, too! That was the best," Iris says.

"Oh, the good old days! The novelty wears off quick," Will says.

"Speaking of the novelty wearing off … we need to talk about Buddy. He's a little different than the other foster babies we've had. He needs extra gentle hands." Now Maxine is the one talking.

"Because he's broken?" Esme asks.

"He's not broken. He has a broken arm and a broken leg." Will's voice is nice.

"And seven broken ribs, but who's counting?" Maxine says that fast and she's so quiet that I don't think anyone heard her except maybe Will, because he gave her a funny look.

"I'd like to break whoever broke him," Theo says. He sounds angry.

"Whoever broke him is broken, too," Will says.

The Mom woman starts talking again. "I need you kids to understand that you can't pick him up unless your dad or I say it's okay. He's been through a lot, and it might be a while before he settles down. We all are going to have to have extra patience."

"I hope he doesn't cry all the time like he did today."

"He might, at least until he feels better and knows he is safe. Remember when the twins were here? They cried for weeks, but it didn't last."

"Oh my gosh, I thought I was going to *die*," Theo says as he covers his ears. "Crying doesn't say half of it. More like screeching!"

"Then there was Jade. She never cried. She was happy all the time."

"Yep, they're all different."

"Okay, so tonight, here's the plan," Maxine says. "After dinner, Theo is getting a ride to basketball. Dad's staying here and I'm going to run to the store and get some things for Buddy."

"Aw, do you have to go tonight? You said you'd help me study for my spelling test," Iris says.

"I'm afraid so. He needs everything, including diapers and pajamas."

"Thank God. What little dude wants to wear a girly T-shirt?" Theo asks.

"For some reason, I doubt he minds," Will says.

"Can I come with you, Mom? Please?" Iris asks.

"Me too?" says Esme.

"Nope," Will says. "You girls are hanging with me and the little man. Iris, I'll quiz you on your spelling words. Mom needs her Target time."

I'm suddenly tired of trying to get the bits of food into my mouth. It's too hard. I'm tired of sitting in this high chair. And tired of these people, too. And I'm hungry.

Without warning, I launch into my next screaming fit.

"Wow, so that's the crying you were talking about," Will says as he stands up and moves toward me. I don't know what kind of hands he has. I don't know if they sizzle.

He reaches down, picks me up, and holds me close. His arms are big but they aren't scary. There's no trace of sizzle.

"I'll make him a bottle. I don't think he knew what to do with that sippy cup." Maxine stands and crosses the room.

"Isn't he a little old for a bottle?"

"Maybe, but that's what he came with. The worker had no idea how or what he's been eating. I guess we'll have to figure it out as we go along. I'll pick up baby food while I'm out." She fills a bottle and hands it to Will.

"Kids, clear the table please." Their voices all start making noise at once. None of them sound happy.

"Seriously, you guys? Is it that hard? It's plates and cups." Will sounds annoyed, but his arms still don't sizzle.

"Fine, fine … I'll do the pots and pans," says Theo. There is laughing. I remember that sound. I like it.

"Wow, what a gesture. Don't overdo it, Theo." More laughing.

I still scream anyway.

CHAPTER 22

MY HEAVY ARM AND LEG don't feel so heavy anymore, even though they still have those big things on them. Esme is sitting on the floor and so am I, my back to her belly. If I lean my head and look way, way up, her long hair tickles my face as she looks down at me.

The toy in her hand is moving back and forth and making happy sounds.

"Here, Buddy. Do you want it? Take it, you can have it." She holds the toy out in front of both of us. I reach for it with my good hand.

"Good job, Buddy!" I shake it up and down like she did, but only for a little bit because it slips out of my hand and onto the floor. She picks it up and holds it out. "Try again, Buddy. You can do it!"

The doorbell rings and Maxine crosses the room.

"I'm so sorry I'm late. I got stuck in court and then I misjudged the time it would take to get here. It's a little further than I thought. I'm Stephanie." I turn my head toward the sound of the voice. I've never seen her before.

"Gosh, no, don't worry about it. I really appreciate you calling to let me know. You might be the first caseworker to ever do that. Please, come in and meet Buddy."

"Buddy? My file says Michael. Is Buddy his nickname?"

"Yes, apparently it has been. I don't know where it came from, but it's the only name he knows."

"Maybe his mom?" Stephanie says. "Not that it really matters …"

"I'm so glad you're here, because I have a lot of questions and there's a lot going on. What happened to Dawn? I left her messages but I never heard back."

"She left the agency. There *is* a lot going on. But first, let me say hello."

Stephanie walks over to me and bends down. I look up at her.

"Well hey there, you must be Buddy. Who's your friend?" She turns to look at Esme.

"I'm Esme. This is his favorite toy." She holds out my new Alex, except my new Alex doesn't look new anymore.

"Wow, he's nice and soft. I can see why this is his favorite. Does he have a name?"

"We call him X because he has this X mark on his back. Besides, Buddy doesn't really talk yet, but he did make a noise once … well, other than all that screaming noise … and it kind of sounded like 'X'. Do you see it?" Esme points to a place on Alex's back.

"I think I do. X is a good name."

"Here Buddy, want your X?" Esme holds it out, but I don't take it. I watch Stephanie instead. I've never seen her before and I don't know why she is here. I study her face and wait to see what she will do next.

Stephanie stands up and turns toward Maxine. Well, sometimes she's Maxine—at least when Will talks to her. She's also Mom, because that's what Theo and Iris and Esme call her. I don't call her anything, because I don't have any words.

"How's he doing?" Stephanie asks.

"It's been three weeks and we're still trying to adjust and get on a schedule. He cries a lot. He cries for the obvious reasons, but sometimes he's fine and then he just starts screaming out of the blue, for no reason. Then he stops."

"Where's your button, Buddy?" Esme asks. She pushes softly on my belly. I look down at her finger, grab it and stick it into my mouth.

"Yuck!" Esme wipes her finger on my shirt.

"When the start/stop screaming happens, usually someone asks who pushed Buddy's button," Maxine explains. "It's become a family joke."

Stephanie laughs. "Do you think the crying is getting any better? Do you think it's related to his injuries?" Stephanie is writing stuff down on paper.

"I don't think he's in pain. We don't know why he does it. I can usually tell the difference between when he needs something or is hurting and when he's just screaming. Honestly, I think he's just letting loose, blowing off some steam."

"What do you do when he cries or screams like that?"

"Well, sometimes I hold him. Sometimes he doesn't want that, so I give him a little space, but I stay nearby. I think once he gets on a schedule and we get his food figured out, he'll feel better."

"What do you mean, 'get his food figured out'?" Stephanie asks.

"His poor little belly is a mess. It's either in knots or he has diarrhea. It's been hard to sort through what he's been fed and what he's used to eating. I don't think he's had much experience with solid food. He probably was mainly on a bottle."

"Has he been to the doctor yet?"

"He saw a pediatrician right after he got here. They said his records and his immunizations are spotty. He's several sets behind. He's started Pediasure to help with weight gain. The doctor said he could stay on a bottle for now while we start introducing new foods. The goal is to have him gaining weight and off the bottle, but he's still adjusting, and I don't want to take the bottle away from him just yet. We do offer him sippy cups, too, to get him used to drinking from a cup. When he's ready," Maxine explains.

"That makes sense. When do you go back to the doctor?"

"We have an appointment next week for a weight check and some shots. I'll be anxious to see what he weighs. I think he's starting to fill out a little bit, which makes me happy."

Esme and I are still sitting on the floor. We spend a lot of time here, and I like that because it is soft. There aren't any little things scurrying around, either. It's never cold and hard, and nothing ever hurts me when I'm on it. I have neat things to hold or chew on or play with, even if I only have one good hand that isn't so good all the time.

I reach for my Alex and my whole body flops forward and I land on my arm with the heavy thing. I don't cry, even though it kind of hurts.

"Are you okay, Buddy?" Esme says. She starts to pick me up, but I don't like it. Maxine stands.

"Esme, how many times do I have to tell you not to pick him up?"

She reaches her arms down to me. Esme looks like she might cry.

"I'm sorry, Mom. I just wanted to help."

"I know, but remember what we talked about. Only Dad or I can pick him up. But thank you for playing with him."

I look from one to the other and then to Stephanie. I might start to cry now. I'm not sure yet. Maxine turns to Stephanie.

"I think he's getting tired," she says. "He's not a good sleeper. He's up several times a night." I lay my head on Maxine's shoulder. Suddenly, I see Iris peeking out from the kitchen. She makes a funny face at me. Stephanie turns her head just in time to see Iris, too.

"Well hello, I'm Stephanie, Buddy's caseworker. I guess you live here." Iris nods her head.

"I'm Iris."

"Iris, nice to meet you." Stephanie turns to Maxine. "I forgot to ask. How many kids do you have?"

"Three. Theo is twelve and he's not home from school yet. Iris is eight and Esme is seven."

"Got it. So, Iris and Esme, how do you think Buddy is doing?"

"He's good," Iris says as she walks toward me. "Hi, Buddy Boy, how was your day?" I don't say anything, but I like that she talks to me anyway, *of course.*

"That's good. Do you mind showing me around a bit? I'd like to see where he sleeps." I think she's talking to Iris and Esme, but she's looking at Maxine.

"I can show you," says Iris.

"I can, too," says Esme.

"You both can show me," Stephanie says.

The girls lead the way with Stephanie following. Maxine and I walk behind them all.

"This is where me and Iris sleep," Esme tells her. Their room has two beds and lots of toys and books and clothes. Stephanie peeks in the door.

"I love the color. Very pretty."

Next, we see Theo's room. It's not as big as Iris's and Esme's room, and it is messy. Dresser drawers are hanging open and there are clothes all over the floor.

"Wow, I don't think I realized what a mess Theo's room is," Maxine says. "Don't hold it against me!"

"No worries. I get it," Stephanie replies.

We walk a little further and Iris opens the door to the room where I sleep. It has two cribs, even though I only sleep in one. It's pretty small but not messy, even though it has stuff in it too like clothes and books and toys.

Right next to my room is where Maxine and Will sleep.

"Buddy's room is small, but Will and I like to have the foster babies closest to us at night," Maxine says.

"How many kids are you licensed to have?" Stephanie asks.

"Just two. If we had a bigger house, we'd take more, but we're tight on space. One of the first workers we had told us we could get several sets of bunk beds and be licensed for more, but that didn't sound right to us. I thought that was kind of weird for her to suggest."

"You'd be surprised at how many foster parents cram as many kids into their house as they can. Some do it for the right reason. Some do it for the money. And sometimes, it's hard to tell which is which."

"I can't imagine anyone fostering for the money. Twenty-seven dollars a day is nothing."

"Well, if a home is licensed for four kids, that's over one hundred dollars a day, or three thousand dollars a month. If you aren't spending it on the kids, it adds up, I guess," Stephanie says.

"I never thought about it that way."

"Well, good!" Stephanie laughs. "I wish nobody did. But some do."

Eventually, we are back in the living room but I don't sit on the floor with Esme or Iris. I sit in Maxine's lap. I like it here. Her hands are gentle and they never hurt. I don't think they will, but I can't be too sure.

Actually, all of the hands in this house are good hands, even though sometimes the little hands bug me. Not a single hand has sizzle. I keep waiting for it, but I haven't felt it. Yet.

Living with these people is very different than where I lived before. Now I always have someone to play with me or be with me, unless I go to sleep. If my arm or leg or belly hurts sometimes, I use my disappearing trick on it—but if I don't, I cry. Then someone will try to make it better, whatever it is.

Maxine and Stephanie keep talking. I just keep sitting here.

"I was reading his file and saw he was due at the orthopedic clinic and should have had the developmental assessment. At least, I'm hoping he did," Stephanie says.

"He did," Maxine is nodding. "He had his follow-up with orthopedic last week. He still has another three weeks or so in both casts."

Stephanie keeps writing.

"We completed part of the developmental assessment. The casts need to be off before they can finish it."

"Does that mean we have to wait another month before he can begin services?"

"No, he has an intake appointment for occupational and speech therapy. They're going to combine both therapies into one session. They'll finish up the full assessment after the casts come off and then start physical therapy after that."

"Good! I can't imagine. He was supposed to be assessed months ago, way before he came here."

"Iris, can you come here?"

"What, Mom?" Iris calls out.

"There's a stack of papers from Children's Hospital on the kitchen counter. Can you bring them here?"

Iris appears with some papers and hands them to Maxine. Maxine shuffles through them with one hand.

"Here are the names and numbers of the therapists he'll be seeing." She pulls a couple of papers from the stack and hands them to Stephanie.

"You read my mind. I was just about to ask you if you had those. Thanks!" Stephanie looks at the papers and writes some things down.

"When we go, I'll ask for a copy of results of the assessments he's already done and send it to you," Maxine offers.

"I'd really appreciate it. Thank you. I'll get it eventually, but if it's not too much trouble and you get it and send it to me, that would really be helpful."

"No problem," Maxine says.

My eyes are heavy. Stephanie and Maxine have been talking for a long time.

"I have some questions for you," Maxine continues.

"Sure, go ahead …"

I guess they're going to keep talking some more.

"What's the plan for Buddy? How long do you think he'll be here? We don't know much about what to expect. So far, he hasn't had any visits with anyone."

"He doesn't have visits with his mom because of the child endangering charge. The judge from criminal court put on a no-contact order. She's out of jail right now with a trial date set for next month."

"Is there any other family? What about his dad?" Maxine asks.

"At this point, the mom says she doesn't know who the biological father is. Her boyfriend at time, Raymond, signed Buddy's birth certificate, even though he's not the biological father."

"You mean he has rights, even if he's not biologically related?"

"Yes, because he signed the birth certificate," Stephanie explains.

"Does he even know Buddy? Did he take care of him?"

"I doubt it. He and mom split up right after Buddy was born. I don't think he's seen Buddy since then. Mom's had no contact with Raymond and says she doesn't know where he is."

"But he still has rights?" Maxine looks totally confused.

"Yeah, he does, because he signed the birth certificate. He's still the legal father, which means he has some rights, so we must consider him for placement."

"Seriously? Just because he signed the birth certificate?" Maxine looks even more confused. I've never seen her look like this. The look on her face reminds me of Dawn, the lady who used to come and see me.

"Yes, seriously. He's been notified of all the court hearings, but he's never attended. He did talk to the previous caseworker one time. He told her he wasn't in a position to take Buddy, but his sister said she'd take him."

"You'd place him with his mom's old boyfriend's sister, just because he signed the birth certificate?" Maxine asks in a voice that makes it sound like she's never heard something so crazy.

"Well, yes, she'd be a consideration. Do you have a problem with kids going to live with relatives?"

Maxine shakes her head.

"No. We've had several foster kids who went to live with relatives after being with us. We still keep in touch with some of them," Maxine says.

"How has that gone for you?" Stephanie asks.

"It's gone all kinds of ways. We had twins who went to their maternal aunt and uncle. We keep in touch with them and they're doing great. One of our foster babies, we had her for eighteen months, she went to back to her grandmother and we never heard from her again. We had siblings, ages two and four. They were reunited with their mom. She worked very hard to get them back, and we wanted to support her, but she wanted a clean break. I have no idea how they are doing. They were with us for more than a year."

"So you're open to contact from relatives?" Stephanie asks.

"Yeah, we always have been—if it makes sense, anyway."

"That's good," Stephanie says. "Sometimes foster parents get an idea that their foster child belongs to them and they do everything they can to sabotage reunification—especially if they went into fostering because they couldn't have biological children."

"Trust me, that's not us." Maxine laughs. "Just look around here. We are definitely not without children."

Stephanie laughs, too.

"So, are you saying you're looking at this guy's sister as a possible placement?"

"Well, no. The old caseworker talked to her and she said she wasn't interested. It's documented in the file. I called her last week to see if she knew how to get a hold of Raymond, because the number I had for him wasn't working. She didn't, and without me asking, she told me again that he wasn't interested in placement. She actually sounded a little annoyed that I called her."

"So, what is the plan?"

"Right now, it's a wait-and-see game. We need to see what happens at Mom's trial next month. She could be found guilty on all charges, sentenced, and transferred to a prison anywhere in the state. She could be eligible for drug treatment in a locked setting, instead. She could get ordered to a facility where Buddy could live with her. We'll just have to see what happens."

"I figured Mom had racked up so many charges that prison was a given," Maxine says.

"In this system, *nothing* is a given. Her charges all stem from substance abuse, so there is a chance she could get diverted from prison and placed in drug treatment instead. The prisons are over-crowded anyway."

There's a pause and no one speaks for a moment.

"We'll know more after Mom's trial," Stephanie says.

"Okay." Maxine takes a deep breath. I can feel it because my head is on her chest. "In the meantime, we'll just keep taking good care of Buddy and do our best to help him catch up. He's pretty much a mess right now."

"Because of his delays?" Stephanie asks.

"Not only that, although that's bad enough. He's been through so much." Maxine's voice is shaky. "Broken bones and ribs. He's been horribly neglected. The back of his head is flat. Emotionally, he seems fragile. He is so guarded, like he's just taking everything in and waiting to see what he thinks about it. I hate that everything is so up in the air for him."

There's another long pause.

"Maybe you see him as a mess, but here's what I see," Stephanie says. "I see a baby who is being well cared for and loved, right this very minute. He's got a team of people who are going to help him get on the right track. I see hope for him, no matter what his future looks like because you are giving him exactly what he needs. He's healing. He won't be a mess forever."

"Here's what we're going to do," she continues. "You let me handle his case. We'll let the therapists do what they do best, and you keep doing what you're doing."

"Okay." Maxine takes another deep breath. "I think we can handle that, can't we girls?" Maxine looks at Iris and Esme, who have been sitting quietly at the other end of the room, watching TV.

"Handle what, Mom?" Esme asks.

"Lovin' on our little Buddy Boy," Maxine says. She holds me just a little tighter and kisses me on my head.

"Well, yeah, of course," Iris says.

"I was just checking to see if you were paying attention."

"Okay, well, it's getting late and I still have another home visit to make." Stephanie puts her papers into her bag and stands up.

"I can't thank you enough. You are the first worker who has ever been so … *good*. It makes everything much easier," Maxine says. She stands with my head resting on her shoulder. I'm almost asleep. "I'll let you know how the appointments go."

"I'm just doing my job," Stephanie says. "Foster parents like you make my job easier, too. Anyway, call me if you need anything. I'm not in the office a lot, but I check my voice mail often throughout the day." Stephanie hands her a card and then reaches out to touch me. "I think you're in a pretty good place, Buddy. What do you think?"

I don't know what I think. I don't think Something Next is coming, but I can never be sure. So far, none of these hands have had sizzle, but I don't know for sure if it will stay that way.

I think I want to sleep.

CHAPTER 23

"IT'S A BIG DAY FOR you, big guy," Maxine says as she unbuckles the straps on my seat and easily slides me out of it, even though the heavy things on my arm and leg could make it hard. She's used to it by now, and I guess I am, too. I'm glad my arm and leg don't hurt nearly as much anymore.

Maxine sets me on her hip and throws my diaper bag over her shoulder.

"This is a big place, but we'll find our way," she says as we enter an elevator. A small person looks up and waves at me. He's smiling. I look away and put my head on Maxine's shoulder. Sometimes I like new faces, but today, not so much.

"Buddy, look, there's a little boy waving at you," Maxine says. "Can you say hi?"

I don't look up.

"What's his name?"

"His name is Buddy," Maxine replies.

"My name is Tyrone. I'm five. I come here a lot. This morning, my baby brother threw up all over the place. It was disgusting! He's not sick, though. I mean, he's just a little sick and it will go away. He doesn't have to come to the hospital or anything. Does Buddy come here a lot?"

"Tyrone, remember, we talked about how it's not polite to ask people questions like that, especially strangers. Not everybody likes to talk as much as you do. This nice lady probably doesn't want to hear about Josh being sick this morning, either." The voice comes from the big person standing next to him.

"I don't mind," Maxine laughs. "Buddy needs a little extra help with things like learning how to talk, so we come here for that. He's not sick. He's just fine. Aren't you, Buddy?" Maxine's hand is on my head. I still don't look up.

"That's good he's not sick, because I was really sick before and that was *horrible*. But I'm better now. Right, Mom?"

"That's right."

The elevator stops with a ding.

"Oncology. Here we are!" Tyrone says as he reaches out for his mom's hand. "Bye, Buddy! Good luck with your talking!"

"Good luck to you, too!" Maxine says as she chuckles. They step out of the elevator and disappear.

"He sure was a friendly little guy. That'll be you soon enough, Buddy, talking up a storm and making all kinds of friends."

The elevator dings again and we step out.

"Looks like we go this way," Maxine says and starts walking.

She talks to a lady behind a desk and then we sit down and wait until another lady calls out a name and Maxine stands.

"This must be Michael," the lady says. She is smiling. I just look at her. I don't like her face, either. It's one of those days. "My name is Teresa. I'm the speech therapist who will be working with you all."

"Nice to meet you," Maxine says. "Michael's nickname is Buddy. Everyone calls him Buddy."

"Okay then, Buddy it is." She bends down a little closer. "Hi, Buddy. I like your shirt. It has dogs on it. Do you like dogs?" I still just look at her.

She walks alongside us, down a hallway and into a room. There are pretty colors everywhere and books and things to play with. "Have a seat," the lady says as she gestures to a chair. Maxine sits down with me on her lap.

"I've had a chance to look over the partial assessments that have already been done. How long has he been in your home?"

"A little over three weeks," Maxine says.

"That's not long."

"Depends on the day," Maxine says, laughing. I like when she laughs. I think about smiling. Nah.

"Why don't you fill me in on the concerns you have about Buddy?"

"Well, regarding his speech, he really doesn't have any," Maxine says. She takes a deep breath. I can feel it.

"Are there any words he uses?"

"Not really."

"Does he make any noise at all, like babbling?"

"No. When he first came, he screamed for hours at a time. That has settled down a lot, but other than that, he's pretty quiet."

"How does he communicate? Does he have different kinds of cries?"

"I can usually tell if he's frustrated or hurt, but it's kind of hard to tell if he's hungry or tired."

There's a knock on the door and a man comes in. He holds his hand out to Maxine.

"Hi, I'm Kyle, the occupational therapist. Sorry, I'm a little late. I just finished up with another client." I don't like his face, either.

"I'm Maxine, Buddy's foster mom. Technically, Michael's foster mom, but everyone calls him Buddy."

"Hi, Buddy." He's looking right at me. I look away. I don't like to look at people I don't know, especially in the eyes.

"Maxine and I were just getting started. Buddy's not using words to communicate. Not yet, anyway." Teresa turns back to me and Maxine. "Does he point or use gestures? Of course, he's only got use of one arm and hand right now …"

Maxine shakes her head. Teresa shuffles through a pile of papers, picks one up and studies it.

"What changes have you noticed in him over in the time he's been with you?"

"Honestly, not that many. He doesn't scream as much as he did the first week. Other than that, he's pretty laid back. He's not very demanding, that's for sure."

"Are there any other children in your home?" Now Kyle is talking. Maxine nods her head.

"There are three. We have a twelve-year-old son and two daughters—seven and eight."

"It probably gets a little busy and hectic in your house at times," Kyle says. Maxine nods her head again.

"How does Buddy do when things are busy? If there's a lot going on, different noises, like doors slamming or kids being loud, does he get upset?"

This time, Maxine shakes her head. "He really doesn't. We've tried to keep things as calm as we can these first few week. Trying to stay on a schedule and lay low for a while, until he settles in more. Of course, there's only so much of that possible with three kids and school and sports and all that. But nothing much seems to bother him. If anything, he could stand to be a little more lively. He's pretty chill."

They keep talking and talking and talking, and I don't think they'll ever stop. They try to talk to me, too, but I decide to pull my disappearing trick instead. I don't like their faces and I don't like this place.

I'm tired, anyway.

When I open my eyes, I'm back home and I hear Maxine and Esme and Iris talking in the other room. I sit in my seat and listen to the sounds coming from the kitchen. The front door opens, and Will walks in.

"Hi, Buds!" he says with a big smile. He reaches in, unbuckles my straps, and pulls me close. "What're you doing in here all by yourself?" He carries me into the kitchen.

"Hi, Dad!" Iris says.

"How's my girls?" Will asks as he kisses both Iris and Esme on their heads.

"Was he awake?" Maxine asks. "I just looked in on him a little bit ago." She leans in to kiss Will and she kisses me, too. I like when she does that.

"He was," Will says. "He still looks sleepy. Rough day?"

"Not really. We had his first appointment with the occupational and speech people today. It went okay. He didn't do much. In fact, he fell asleep there. Out like a light. He's going to need a diaper change."

"I'll change him. I want to change out of my clothes, too." Will carries me down the hall. I love that his hands never have sizzle.

When we return to the living room, Theo is playing a game on the television. Will plops down on the couch and I settle into his lap.

"Does he need a bottle?" Will calls out.

"I'm on it," Maxine calls back while walking into the room with a bottle in her hand. She sits down next to us.

"Here you go, Buddy." Will holds my bottle while I drink it. I used to be able to hold it by myself, but not anymore, not since the heavy thing came on my arm.

"What did the people have to say today?"

"Well," Maxine says, "he's very delayed."

"And what did Buddy have to say about that?"

"Very funny."

"Buddy thought it was. Right, Buddy?" I pause from my bottle, look up, and smile at him. It's the first time I smile today. He laughs. "Told ya!" Maxine isn't laughing, though. "I'm sorry. Tell me more. What do we need to do?"

"For starters, weekly speech therapy and occupational therapy. The more we talk to him, the better."

"Esme alone has that covered!" Will laughs again. "What else did they have to say?"

"Well, a lot of the things they suggested we already do, like get him on a schedule, talk to him a lot, wait for and encourage him to answer, read books, play, that sort of thing. Expose him to different things." Maxine pauses.

"I do think it's good for him to be here with the kids. He needs more stimulation, and here, he gets plenty of stimulation. I just wish he would be more engaged." I look closely at Maxine's face. Her eyes look sad.

"I know you're worried about him." Will puts his hand on Maxine's arm. "But I'm not."

"How can you not be worried about him? He doesn't babble or coo or anything. He doesn't look up when you say his name. He hardly makes eye contact. God only knows if he can even roll over, thanks to the broken ribs and bones." Tears are running down Maxine's cheeks.

"You know why I'm not worried about him? First, because well, that doesn't do any good. Second, he's making progress. Maybe he's not moving much and he's probably not going to, at least until he heals. But look what he does now. Just look. Buddy, show Mom your smile and make her feel better."

I just stare at him.

"Come on, I know you've got one in there somewhere. I just saw it a minute ago. Where you hiding it?"

I love when people talk to me, especially when they make funny faces at the same time, like Will is doing right now. I smile.

"See? I told you! He didn't smile for at least the first week." Will and Maxine both laugh. My smile gets bigger.

"I guess I forgot. You're right. We'll just take it one step at a time."

"There you go again, getting ahead of yourself." Will chuckles as he rearranges me on his lap.

"You are such a dork," Maxine groans.

"Yep, and you wouldn't have me any other way." He leans over and kisses her. Then he kisses me on the top of my head.

I hope Something Next never comes.

CHAPTER 24

A VISITOR IS HERE TO SEE me. She has a big, black bag on her shoulder. I think I've seen her before, but maybe not.

"Hi, Buddy! You got your casts off!" she says when Maxine opens the door with me in her arms. I love that she talks to me. The visitor reaches out for my hand and gives in a tiny shake. "You're free!"

She's right. No more heavy things on my arm and leg anymore. They move around a lot now.

"Say hi, Stephanie," Maxine says with a big smile. She's talking to me, too. They're both looking at me. I just look from one to the other and smile, and then bury my head in Maxine's shoulder. "Come on in."

"Wow, he looks great!" Stephanie says as she follows us across the living room. Maxine sits on the couch with me on her lap while Stephanie takes a seat across the room.

"He's doing really well," Maxine says. Her hand runs across the top of my head. Her smile stretches across her face, almost all the way to her ears. I love when she smiles like that. I look up and lock my eyes on hers. I could look at her eyes all day. Sometimes I wish I could jump inside them and stay there forever. I'd feel good inside there. Forever.

My own eyes watch everything. They always have. They watch doors open and close. They watch for things to move fast. They watch people, especially hands and faces. I don't look in eyes, though. I don't know what will be there and I don't want to know. I'll look in Maxine's eyes, but that's it.

"He's been here what, two months?" Stephanie asks. She's looking down at paper in her lap. All my visitors always have lots of papers.

"Closer to ten weeks," Maxine tells her.

"When did the casts come off?"

"A couple of weeks ago."

"How'd he do?"

"Actually, it was a little strange. As soon as we walked into the orthopedic clinic, he got very still and very quiet and he stayed that way. Even when the casts came off. Then he fell asleep as soon as we left and he was out for hours."

"Hmmm, that is interesting." Stephanie is writing on a pad of paper. "I've heard a healed broken bone can hurt a lot when a cast first comes off, because it's been immobile. Stiff and painful. I've never had a broken bone, but that's what I've heard."

"Yeah, the doctor told us to be sure and give him Tylenol before we brought him in for his appointment. Give it a chance to kick in. I think it helped."

"I just got the initial reports from speech, occupational, and physical therapy. Wow, he has a lot of goals. And a lot of appointments. I bet it's keeping you busy," Stephanie says.

Maxine nods. "Yep, speech is Tuesdays and Thursdays. Physical therapy Mondays and Wednesdays. OT is every Wednesday."

"Wow, that's a loaded schedule. And you're able to get him to all of those appointments?"

"Will takes him sometimes if he's off work."

"Thank you, from the bottom of my heart, for transporting him to all those appointments. If I had to do that, I don't know what I'd do. It would be impossible."

"Of course we'd transport him. I can't imagine expecting you or someone from the county to do that. Besides, Kyle and Teresa and Katie … she's the physical therapist … they tell me what to work on at home, and I can tell them how he's doing. It's a team effort: all of us. I wouldn't want to miss that."

"Yeah, but not all foster parents and relatives see it like you do. If they won't or can't take them, it falls on the worker, since the county has custody."

"Well, don't worry about Buddy. We'll get him where he needs to be."

"Speaking of where he needs to be …" Stephanie pauses.

"What?" Maxine asks.

"Some other placement options have come up. Mom was in court last week for her criminal case. She pled guilty on the child endangering charge and drug possession. In exchange, the prosecutor dropped the resisting arrest and disorderly conduct. She's going to serve six months on both charges."

"So she's not an option for reunification?" Maxine asks.

"No, she's not. But the legal father has changed his mind. He's requesting visits."

"Is that the guy who was mom's boyfriend and signed the birth certificate, even though he's not the biological father?"

"Yes. Raymond Morris."

There's a long pause. I look in Maxine's eyes, but she's not looking in mine. Her eyes are far away.

"Okay, well, so when do visits start? Let me guess. Tomorrow?"

"No," Stephanie laughs. "Spoken like a veteran foster parent."

"Sorry, I couldn't resist." Maxine laughs, too. "That's the way it usually happens."

"Not if I can help it. I'm not just going to agree to turn Buddy's days upside down without more information first. Raymond is entitled to visits, but he's been MIA until now, and I want to understand who he is, his intentions, all that."

"Well then, you're the first caseworker I've ever met who thinks that way. When do you think visits will start?" Maxine asks.

"I'm not sure. I want to meet with him first, and he's supposed to get back with me about his schedule. Hopefully, he'll let me know sooner rather than later."

"That sounds like a plan," Maxine says. "I like plans."

"Me too," Stephanie says. "I'm not a fan of haphazard. I like to avoid it when I can, although it's not always possible."

I sit quietly on Maxine's lap while they trade words back and forth until the sound of the school bus beeps outside and the front door flies open. The kids pile in, dropping backpacks on the floor.

"We're home," they yell before heading straight to the kitchen.

"Looks like it's about to get busy around here," Stephanie says. She gathers up her papers and her big, black bag.

"Kids, come and say hello to Buddy's worker," Maxine calls out. One by one, they appear then disappear and later, Stephanie and her big, black bag head out the front door.

"Buddy, you are such a good boy." Maxine kisses me on the top of my head. I look up at her and smile. We lock eyes again.

I wish I could jump into them and stay there.

CHAPTER 25

I WAKE UP TO SMELLS THAT make my belly rumble. I love when I wake up to these smells. Usually, it doesn't smell like this in the morning. If it does, it's on a day when nobody goes to school.

Lots of days and nights have passed since I came to live here. So many, I don't even know how many. Lots and lots.

I lay in my crib quietly with X and look at the ceiling. I move my head back and forth, back and forth and listen for the *swish swish* sound like I do every morning until someone comes to get me.

Sometimes it's Maxine or Will. Sometimes it's Theo or Iris or Esme. No matter who it is, I'm happy when they come. I like to wake up in the morning and see who's going to come to get me. Mornings are a happy time.

Until now.

Suddenly, there is screaming and it scares me. I freeze. I don't move even a finger. I've never heard it before and I don't know what it is.

I hear fast footsteps across the floor and Maxine swings open the door to my room.

"Shhh, shhh, it's okay, Sweetie Pie. I've got you." She reaches into the other crib and pulls someone out. It's a she, and I don't even know where she came from.

I pull myself up with my two good hands and stand. I can even do it while I'm holding X. It's my new trick. I learned it after the heavy things on my arm and leg went away.

I get my first good look at this person in Maxine's arms. She's bigger than me but a lot littler than Theo and Iris and Esme. And she's in my space. I'm the only one who goes in Maxine's arms. Everybody knows that. Well, at least Iris and Esme and Theo know that, because they never go in Maxine's arms. It's *my* space.

She keeps screaming, even though Maxine is holding her and talking softly. I'm the only one who does the screaming around here, and I don't even do it as much as I did before.

There's only one thing to do at a time like this. Scream louder than her. So I do.

"Goodness, Buddy, not you, too! You always wake up happy." Maxine turns around with the girl in her arms.

Would you be happy if some screaming girl was in your space?

"Come here, you." Maxine reaches in and with one arm, she pulls me onto her other hip. I wrap my legs around her and cling tightly to her shirt with one fist. I used to dangle when she picked me up, but I don't do that anymore. I can hold on now. It's another one of my new tricks.

The Screamer and I are face-to-face while Maxine carries us both into the kitchen. Will is standing at the stove where all the yummy smells are coming from.

"Which one do you want?" Maxine asks. Will holds out his hands and I dive toward them to get away from that screaming girl. In all the time I've been here, Will's hands have never once had sizzle. Not one time, and I'm in his arms every day.

"I guess I'm taking Buddy Boy," he says. He doesn't seem to mind.

All at once, Iris and Esme scramble from their seats and crowd around Maxine with the girl in her arms.

"Hi, baby girl, what's your name? Where'd you come from?"

The girl stops crying and looks from one face to another. She wiggles out of Maxine's arms, so Maxine puts her down on the floor. She stands on both feet, walks over to the bench at the kitchen table and climbs onto it.

I cannot believe she can do that trick. Iris and Esme return to their seats at the table, too.

"Well, I'll be darned. Look at her go," Maxine says as she helps the girl sit in a little seat on top of the bench. I don't even know where that little seat came from. It wasn't here before.

"Hey guys, this is Gabby. She came in the middle of the night."

"Mom, she stinks," Theo says.

"You're right. She does. As soon as her belly is full, she'll get a bath."

"Why didn't you give her a bath when she got here?" Theo asks.

"Have you ever had a bath in the middle of the night?" Maxine asks.

"No, but did I ever need one in the middle of the night?"

"Okay, you have a point. But how would you like to be little and taken to a strange house in the middle of the night, half asleep, and dumped into bathtub under bright lights? I bet you wouldn't like that. Wouldn't you rather wake up on your own with the smell of bacon and eggs and pancakes cooking?"

"Well, yeah," Theo says. "We should eat like this every morning."

"Don't count on it," Will laughs.

"Hi, Gabby!" Esme says. "Are you hungry?" Gabby stares at her with giant eyes then grabs a fistful of pancakes off Esme's plate.

"Mom!" Esme is mad.

"I'm sorry, honey. She doesn't know better." Maxine puts a small plate with cut up pancakes and bacon on the table in front of Gabby. "Here's yours, Gabby."

"Theo, grab Buddy's sippy cup out." Theo pulls my sippy cup from the refrigerator. I reach out for it and take a drink. It's another one of my new tricks. I have so many, it's hard to keep count.

Will hands me to Theo, who straps me into my high chair.

Gabby crams the food into her mouth.

"Whoa, slow down, Sweets." Will pulls the plate away and sits down next to her. She starts crying. My lip starts to quiver.

"It's okay, we're just going to take a bite at a time." Will's voice is nice. I'm glad his hands don't sizzle or they would definitely have sizzle now. My lip quivers some more.

"Buddy Boy, you're fine," Maxine says gently. She sits down next to my high chair and puts a pancake and banana on my tray. I've gotten much better at using my hands to get food into my mouth, but I don't pick this food up because I'm still holding X and because my lip is still quivering. "Aww, is she scaring you? There's nothing to be afraid of. She's just a little girl."

She's not scaring me. I just don't like her in my house.

Maxine turns toward Will.

"I'm glad Buddy had a chance to settle in before the next kid came along. He's come so far," Maxine says.

"He has! Hardly looks like the same kid. I wonder what he thinks of his new friend. It's been a while since we had two this close in age," Will responds.

"Not quite a year apart," Maxine says.

"She seems so much older than Buddy. One bite at a time, Gabby," Will says. "Are you thirsty? Take a drink." He holds a sippy cup out to her. She reaches for it and sucks it down.

"She does seem a lot older, but I guess she would. She's very advanced. Not many three-year-olds can wander off in the middle of the night and walk into a bar. Alone and with a bucket on her head, no less. That takes talent."

"Ain't that crazy?" Will is shaking his head. "I could not believe it when the worker told us that. How in the world does a toddler wander away at two a.m. and end up in a bar? I can't believe she didn't trip. Or fall. Or stumble into traffic. Or get killed. *With a bucket on her head!* Amazing. Things like this make me think these kids are miracles. Really."

"Well, I'm sure she had a guardian angel on her shoulder," Maxine says. "For as heartbreaking as it is, it's a good thing she wandered out of that house. Who knows how long she'd been left alone? Besides, at least she stumbled into a safe place."

"At least someone there was sober enough at two a.m. to call 911."

"True. Did you see the snippet on the news this morning? They left out the part about the bucket."

"You mean the news that didn't make the news?" Will laughs. "Yeah, I noticed."

"I'm so glad you are home today," Maxine says.

"Me too, it's good timing. I do have to run down to the firehouse to pick something up, but I can take one or both of them with me."

Gabby must be done eating because she is already climbing out of her seat.

"She's on the move, that's for sure." Will stands and follows that running girl into the other room.

I just munch on my pancake and smile at Maxine. She's all mine now and nobody is in her arms.

"And how's my sweet boy this morning?" She smiles too and rubs my head. I smile bigger.

"Now, don't you get any wrong ideas about sharing a bedroom with a girl, especially when she's older than you!" Maxine laughs.

I laugh, too, because she does.

CHAPTER 26

IT'S QUIET IN THE CAR since it's only me and Will and X. When the other kids are here, it can be loud, because they all talk a lot. Most of the time, I like to listen to the talking, but it's also nice to just sit here in my big car seat, looking out the window with only the sound of music. Will likes music. Sometimes his head moves back and forth the littlest bit when it's playing. So I move my head back and forth just a little bit. Like he does.

The car stops for good and Will gets me out of my seat. Right away, I see the big, red firetrucks and point to one. I've been here before. I like this place.

"Truck. That's right, Buddy Boy. Big, red truck."

"Hey, big guy and little man, whatcha doin' here today?" A man walks toward us with a big smile on his face. He is always smiling. He rides on firetrucks, just like Will does.

"Grabbing some gear. I took a shift at Station 29 tomorrow." With me still in his arms, Will walks toward the place where he keeps his fireman things.

"Well, hand the little man over while you gather your stuff, then." The man holds out his hands.

"You wanna go to Bob for a minute?" I look at Will, then at Bob, then back at Will and lay my head on Will's shoulder.

"Not today? Okay, that's fine," Will tells me.

"What's the matter, Buddy? You like your old friend Bob." Bob still has that big smile on his face, but I don't smile back.

I do like Bob, and I love to go to the firehouse. People here are always happy to see me.

I don't answer him because for one, I don't feel like it, and for two,

I don't use words.

"Aw, Buddy's just having a rough day. We took in another foster child last night. A little girl. Buddy's not real sure what to think of her just yet."

"Well shoot, could you blame him? Another girl in the house? I feel for ya, little man." Bob laughs a loud laugh and Will laughs, too.

He gathers his big, heavy fireman coat and hat and so much other stuff that it takes us two trips to get it to the car, because he keeps one arm just for me.

"You seen the chief?" Will asks.

"Yup, in his office."

Will and I go to the kitchen to look for Chief. He's sitting behind a big desk.

"Hi, Will, what's up? I see you got your little guy with you. Hi, Buddy! Holy smokes, boy, you're getting so big I hardly recognized you." I smile at him. Everybody here knows my name and they all talk to me, which I love, *of course*.

"I wanted to ask you if there's any way I can get coverage for a shift next week. Maxine and I just found out there's a court hearing on Buddy's case, and I'd really like to be there. It's not mandatory for me to go, but I think it's really important."

"That's going to be tough for us to figure out on such short notice, especially with being down one guy already," Chief says.

"I know," Will says while he shifts me from one arm to the other.

"But, like I said before, what you got going on right here is just as important. We'll make it work."

"Thanks, Chief," Will says.

"So, did you see the news about that little girl who wandered alone into that bar last night?" Chief asks as he stands up and walks toward us.

"Not only did I see the news, but I saw the little girl, too. In fact, she's at home with Maxine right now."

"No kidding? Good for you. She's a lucky little thing to land in your home."

"I don't know if 'lucky' is the word I'd use to describe any child whose parents didn't take care of them," Will says.

"You know what I mean. You're a good man to take these kids in. They're blessed to be in your family. How long have you had Buddy now?"

"About four months," Will replies.

"Is that all? Unbelievable. He was such a pathetic little thing when you first got him. Just look at him now. He's really growing. He'll be eating you out of house and home before too long." Chief is laughing.

"He's growing by leaps and bounds, that's for sure. We just hope to keep it that way."

"Well, we hope so, too," Chief says.

"Alright, well, Buddy and I are gonna run now. We gotta get Theo from basketball and hit the grocery. Thanks for covering for me next week so I can go to court. I really appreciate it," Will says as he holds out his hand.

"Of course. Anything for our Buddy Boy," Chief says as he shakes Will's hand then reaches out for mine.

"Give me five, Buddy." I reach out and hit his hand with mine. It's another new trick.

CHAPTER 27

"I AM EXHAUSTED," MAXINE SAYS to Will as he hands me over to her. Where did X go? I look all around, but I don't see her, so I make the noise I make when I want my X.

"Daddy will get her, don't worry," Maxine says.

Will and Theo disappear outside and return carrying bags into the kitchen. Will hands me X. I must have left her in the car.

"Girls!" Will yells. "Come help unload."

"Shhhh!!" Maxine says. "Gabby is finally down for a nap. I might die if she wakes up right now."

"She never slept all afternoon?" Will asks. Maxine shakes her head.

"She's been going full force. Even the girls need a break from her."

Iris and Esme appear in the kitchen and start rooting through the grocery bags.

"You bought *Berry* Captain Crunch instead of Captain Crunch? I *hate* Berry Captain Crunch. It's not fair!" Iris looks like she's going to cry.

"Pick 'em out," Theo tells her. "No big deal. Don't be such a baby."

"I'm not a baby. In case you didn't notice, there are enough babies around here!!" Iris turns and stomps out of the kitchen.

"Iris, honey, come here," Maxine calls after her.

"Dad, did you get me a poster board for my Social Studies project?" Esme asks as she puts cartons of milk in the refrigerator.

"Shoot, I forgot." Will takes a deep breath. "I'm sorry."

"That was the one thing I told you to make sure you *didn't* forget," Maxine says. She's not happy.

In fact, nobody's happy.

"Esme, here, will you take Buddy? I need to talk to Iris."

"Sure, Mom." Esme reaches her arms out to me and I lean toward her with X in my hand.

"Hey, Buddy. Wanna sit with me and watch some TV?" She carries me into the other room and we sit together on the couch.

I like sitting here with Esme. It's very cozy. With my body up against hers and her arm around my shoulders, my eyes eventually get heavy and I fall asleep.

"Dinner!" Will calls. My eyes open wide and I rub them with both hands.

"Let's go, Buds," Esme says as she picks me up from the couch.

She's back. That screaming girl who was in my room this morning when I woke up. She's right here, sitting in that seat on the bench next to Iris. I forgot about her.

"I didn't know we were having pizza," Esme says as she takes a slice from a big box on the table.

"We always have pizza on New Kid Night," Iris says.

"I figured since Dad went to the grocery, we were having something else."

"More!" Gabby says as she stuffs a bunch of cut-up pieces of pizza into her mouth. She uses two hands. I only use one hand when I put things into my mouth.

"One bite at a time," Maxine tells her in a nice voice as she moves Gabby's plate off to the side. Gabby starts screaming.

"It's okay. You don't need to scream." Maxine takes two bite-size pieces from her plate and Gabby grabs them and shovels them into her mouth.

"More!" she says again. Maxine keeps feeding her two bites at a time. Nobody's feeding me bites at a time. I can feed myself now.

"So, how was everybody's day?" Will asks as he takes a big bite of pizza.

"Good. Monique asked if I could come home from school with her tomorrow. Can I?" Iris asks.

"That's fine with me. Did she ask her dad?" Maxine asks.

"She told me she did."

"Okay, I'll just text him to make sure. Theo, how was your Science test?"

"Eww, that's right! You had a test on worms today! I forgot!" Esme says. She giggles.

"Not just worms. *Segmented worms*. Very important. I'm sure that information will come in handy. Someday. Maybe."

"Here, Buddy, want my sausage?" Iris asks. I love sausage. I nod my head and she puts some on my tray.

"Speaking of worms, it's a beautiful night to be outside," Maxine says.

"What exactly does being outside have to do with worms?" Theo asks.

"Well, worms are outside … and I think we should be, too. Let's go on a walk after dinner. I could use the sunshine and our new little friend could probably run off some steam."

"Can I ride my bike?" Esme asks.

"Sure."

After dinner, Theo buckles me into a stroller and off we go. Iris and Esme ride bikes while Will pushes me in my stroller. Maxine walks with us. Screaming Girl and Theo are way ahead, but I can still see them.

I love being outside. There are so many things to look at that sometimes, I don't know where to look first. I turn my head from side to side and hold onto X while I listen for the *swish swish*. It sounds different in my stroller, but I don't know why.

Will and Maxine walk much slower than the kids, and they stop and talk to the people who live in the houses around us. Lots of people are outside on a night like tonight. I like to see their faces and they always talk to me, *of course*.

"Hey there, looks like you're lagging behind your kiddos. Is that on purpose?" It's the man who lives down the street.

"You got it." Will laughs. We stop moving. I bounce up and down in my stroller.

"Hey, Buddy, when are you gonna go run with those big kids?" he asks.

"Won't be long now. Buddy, do you want to get out and show Mr.

Carson how big you've gotten?" I put my arms up and Maxine reaches in, unbuckles, and pulls me out.

She sets me down on the sidewalk and I stand on both legs. But that's all I do, until I see small things scurry on the ground. They scare me, and I start to cry.

"What's wrong, Buddy?"

I scream louder and cling to Maxine's leg. She picks me up and I am glad. I lay my head on her shoulder and cry and cry and cry some more. I don't like those little scurry things.

"My goodness, what on earth?" Mr. Kemper says. He reaches out a hand to me. "What's the matter, little fella?"

"He's a little temperamental today. New competition in the house, if you know what I mean," Will says as he nods his head toward the kids.

"I thought I saw an extra one. Another foster kid?"

"Yep. Came last night. She's going to keep us on our toes," Maxine says simply. She kisses me on my head. I stop crying. In the distance, I see Theo chasing Gabby and I can hear her laughing from all that way.

I watch her run and run and run. I watch as Theo laughs, too, and stays close beside her. Esme and Iris ride their bikes in circles near them. They are all happy.

Maybe they are happy because they can run and ride bikes and be bigger than me. I want to squirm out of Maxine's arms and run with them, but I don't know how. Besides, there are little scurry things down there; not many, but a few, and that's more than enough for me.

"How long is this one staying?" Mr. Kemper asks.

"No idea. Maybe we'll know more soon," Will says. Mr. Kemper shakes his head.

"I'll tell you what. Shame on those people for having kids and not raisin' 'em. I don't know how you do it. I could never take in some-body else's kids," the old man says.

"Well now, Mr. Kemper, if we didn't, who would?" Will smiles politely.

"I guess. All I'm sayin' is, it's gotta be hard, never knowing who's coming and going."

"Well, yeah, it is hard, but not harder than being a kid with no one to take care of you."

"You're a good family. World needs more of you. Heck, I'm too old to take in a bunch of kids. But I sure do enjoy watching them grow."

The kids are barreling toward us on bikes and feet. Gabby is holding Theo's hand. I don't like that. I wish Theo held my hand.

"Dad, we came up with a new name for her," Theo says. All the kids are smiling.

"Chase. Her nickname should be Chase. Can you guess why?"

"Because she's so FAST! Isn't that a great name for her?" Esme is beaming.

I don't know why they are all laughing. I make the noise I make when I want my X and Iris reaches into the stroller and hands her to me. I rub her against my cheek. It makes me feel better.

"Yes, that's a perfect nickname," Maxine says. "What does she think?"

They all look at Gabby. Her smile is so big, it makes me smile, even though I'm not sure I like her and I don't know where she came from.

"I guess we didn't get too far on our walk," Will says. He pulls a phone from his pocket and looks at it. "And I forgot I have to go back to the store for poster board."

"I have some poster board left over from a garage sale. Didn't make as many signs as I thought I would. It's white. Can you use it?" Mr. Kemper asks.

"I can use it. I need it for my Social Studies project," Esme says.

"Well, good. Wouldn't want it to go to waste," Mr. Kemper says. "You all wait right here and I'll go fetch it."

Mr. Kemper disappears and while we wait, I look down at Gabby. She is standing on the ground and there's a scurry thing near her foot. She doesn't even care or look scared.

I look at her for a little while longer and start to squirm.

"You wanna get down?" Maxine asks.

Maxine sets me down on my two legs. I'm standing, just like Gabby. I hold onto Maxine's finger and take one little step toward the girl. Then I take one more before I stop and look up at all the faces.

"Yeah, Buddy! You just took your first steps!" Theo yells. They all start clapping. I grin from ear to ear and bounce up and down while holding onto Maxine's finger.

"I'm so proud of you, Buddy! Good job!" Maxine bends down and hugs me tight. I throw my arms around her neck and she scoops me up.

"High five, Big Guy," Will says. He holds his hand out to me and I slap it. Maxine sets me back down on my feet and I do it again. More clapping.

Mr. Kemper returns with a big, blank, white poster in one hand.

"Here you go, good as new," Mr. Kemper says. Esme begins to take it, but she's on her bike, so Will reaches out for it instead.

"Thank you," Esme says.

"And thanks for saving me a trip," Will adds.

"Any time, happy to help."

"Okay, kiddos, let's call it a day. We still have homework and baths."

"And hopefully an early bedtime …" Maxine adds as she reaches out for Gabby's hand. "At least for some of us."

CHAPTER 28

THIS MORNING IS *NUTS*! I sit in my high chair with X and watch the flurry of activity around me. Gabby sits in her seat, too, but she's too busy eating to watch everything like I do.

"You've got five minutes until the bus comes and I can't drive you to school today," Maxine calls out to Esme, whose head is under a couch in the living room. She's looking for a shoe. She is crying.

"I can't find it anywhere!" Esme screams.

"This is why I tell you to get your things together before you go to bed. Iris, help your sister find her shoe." Maxine is pulling food out of the refrigerator and loading up lunchboxes. The toaster beeps and two waffles pop up.

"Just wear your other ones. What's the big deal?"

"I can't! I have gym today!"

I turn my head all the way around when I hear a THUMP hit the floor. It's the missing shoe.

"Found it," Theo calls out. Esme rushes over, slides her foot into the shoe's toe, and hops away while pulling on the back.

"Theo, do me a favor. Will you butter those waffles and give them to Buddy? He's been waiting."

"Sure, Mom." When he finishes, he begins to walk toward me, but Iris comes barreling around the corner and crashes straight into Theo. One waffle goes flying. He puts the other on my tray.

"Uh-oh," I say.

"What'd you say, Buddy?? Did you say 'uh-oh'?" Theo is staring at me. They are all staring at me. I look at one face, then another, then another, and say it again.

"Uh-oh!"

Suddenly, there's no more chaos. There's just happiness. Even Gabby is laughing, but she does that a lot.

Except at night. Sometimes when we are in our cribs and waiting to fall asleep, I hear Gabby say very quietly, 'uh-oh'. She says it over and over again, so I started saying it, too. Sometimes, we take turns.

"Good job, Buddy, you said your first word!" Iris and Esme both give me big kisses.

"Okay guys, out the door. Go do good today," Maxine says to the big kids as they dart out of the kitchen.

All different voices shout "Love you" as the front door slams shut.

"Good morning!" Will calls as he comes through the front door, right after the kids leave. He glances around the kitchen. "Looks like a tornado went through here."

"The morning was a little rough. I thought you'd be home by now."

"I know, I'm sorry. We had a late run this morning. But don't worry, I just need some coffee and a shower and I'll be good to go." He gives Maxine a quick kiss on the cheek. "Is anything else wrong?"

Maxine shakes her head.

"No. I'm just on edge because of court today. Guess what? Buddy said his first word. The kids were so excited, you'd have thought we won the lottery. It was the sweetest thing."

"Buddy said his first word? I don't believe it!" Will bends down until his face is right in front of mine. "Alright, let's hear it, Buds. Show me whatcha got." I just smile.

"Nothin'? You got nothing for me?" Now I giggle.

The doorbell rings.

"Good Lord, why on earth would your mother ring the doorbell?" Maxine looks at the clock. "What's she doing here so early, anyway? I thought we had another hour before she got here."

The doorbell rings again.

"Who knows?" Will says as he strolls toward the door and swings it open. Then he stops suddenly.

"Can I help you?"

Maxine looks up from the kitchen sink.

"Hello, are you Mr. Jackson?"

"Yes, what can I do for you?"

"My name is Brenda Wiseman. I'm the caseworker for Gabby Cunningham."

"You gotta be freakin' kidding me," I hear Maxine whisper as she looks around the kitchen and dumps a bunch of dishes in the sink.

"We're in here," she calls out. Her eyes scan the room and land on the flying waffle. With one quick move, she kicks it under the stove so no one can see it any more.

"Uh-oh," I say again. I don't think anyone heard me except maybe Gabby, because then she says it, too.

"Brenda? Hi, I'm Maxine. I thought you were coming tomorrow." Maxine is using her nice voice, but I don't think she's happy.

Brenda opens her bag, pulls out a book, and looks at it.

"Oh, you're right. I thought it was today. Got my days mixed up. Well, since I'm here, I might as well stay. I won't be long. Just need to see her, and then I'll be on my way."

Will and Maxine stare at Brenda. Gabby throws her sippy cup across the room. I just keep munching on my breakfast.

"Gabby, no. We don't throw things," Maxine says as she crosses the room to pick up the cup. "Are you finished eating? You can get down."

Will pushes the table away from the bench and Gabby climbs down. She bolts from the kitchen and Will and Brenda follow her into the living room. I eat all the food on my tray while Maxine stands at the sink and loads the dishwasher.

From the other room, we can hear them talking. I can tell by the sounds that Gabby is playing with blocks. Sometimes she throws them.

When Maxine is finished, she wipes my face and hands and pulls me from my high chair. In the other room, we sit next to Will on the couch.

"Honey, Brenda here was just filling me in on the details of Gabby's case. She's been her caseworker for a while."

"You have? I didn't know she had an open case before she came into care."

Brenda nods her head.

"She sure did. Been open for about six months. I've had it for about four. Domestic violence and substance abuse. Mom also had a previous history with the agency. She has four other kids. I set her up with parenting classes and a drug assessment, but she hasn't gone."

"Four other kids? Where are they?" Maxine looks stunned.

"All adopted out before Gabby was born."

"Did the agency know this? How could they let her take a baby home if she couldn't keep her older kids?"

"You know how it is. Can't take away everybody's kid just because they have a history. As long as they aren't abused or neglected, anyway. Hospital social worker called it in when she was born, but a worker made a home visit and then closed the case. Came back open six months ago."

"Wait a minute. Back up. Isn't there a law that says if someone loses custody of their children and then has another child, Children's Services can automatically file for termination of parental rights? I'm almost sure there's a law that says that."

"Oh, there is, but nobody follows that law."

While they are talking, I start squirming, so Maxine sets me down on the floor with X and I play with a big, soft book. When I look up, Gabby is right in my face. She scares me. Then she takes X and throws her across the room.

All of the sudden, my whole body goes haywire. I start screaming and screaming and screaming, so hard I can barely breathe.

"Oh my goodness, Buddy, what's wrong?" Will jumps up and lifts me from the floor. I scream louder. I don't want him touching me.

Gabby starts screaming, too. Maxine picks her up and holds her. Gabby stops screaming, but I don't, even though Will has X in his hand now and is trying to give it to me.

"Wow, that baby is something else. Spoiled, if you ask me," Brenda says as she shakes her head.

"Well, nobody asked you," Maxine snaps. Will looks shocked. Brenda does, too.

"Excuse me?"

"I said, nobody asked you." Maxine's voice is not happy. Her eyes have water in them.

There's a long pause. I just keep screaming.

"Look, you show up here unannounced, saying things like 'nobody follows the law,' and then you offer opinions we are not interested in hearing. It's not okay. You need to go. Please. Can we just reschedule this visit?" Water is flowing down Maxine's cheeks.

"We have custody of her, which means I'm essentially her legal custodian as long as I'm assigned to her case. I can see her anytime I want." Brenda is angry.

"And you wonder why you never have enough good foster parents, when you treat them like this." Maxine is not using her nice voice.

"Alright." Will puts one hand in the air as if to stop something while he holds me in his other arm. "Let's all take a minute here. Brenda, this is just a terrible time for you to visit. I'm a firefighter and I just got off a forty-eight-hour shift. Gabby's only been here a week and we are all adjusting. My wife hasn't slept much and neither have I. We also have a court hearing on the baby's case in a couple of hours. There's probably not a worse morning for you to knock on the door unexpectedly at eight a.m."

"Well, I'm sorry about that, but I hope you understand that I have twenty-seven cases. I don't have time to come all the way back out here just because I mixed up the days. By the way, why do you need to go to the baby's court hearing? Foster parents never go."

"We always go to court on our foster kids' cases, so we can answer questions about how they are doing. Besides, our caseworker Stephanie said it was good if we could come. She's really good. Do you know her? Her name is Stephanie Hawkins."

"Yeah, I know her. I'm just saying it's unusual for foster parents to come to court. Personally, I don't see the point."

It's quiet for a minute and Maxine is holding her lips together. I can't tell if she's trying not to say something or trying to keep the water from spilling out of her eyes. Finally, Will uses his nice voice.

"Anyway, now that you've seen Gabby, what else do you need

from us in order to finish up? Do you need to take a look around the house? See where she sleeps? What can we do to help you accomplish what you need to get done?"

"I don't need to see where she sleeps." Brenda stands up suddenly. Will looks surprised.

"You don't? I thought that was a rule. Never mind. Okay then, what can we do to help you accomplish what you need to get done?"

"Nothing, I guess."

"Why don't we set up a time for you to come out, whenever it's convenient for you and when things aren't so crazy for us? What's your schedule like next week?"

"Oh, I won't be out here for at least another month to six weeks. I only need to come once a month."

"Do you want to schedule that visit now?"

"No. No idea what my schedule will look like that far out. I'll call you."

They keep talking while Will walks out the door and onto the porch. He is still holding me, but I pull my disappearing trick and pretend everything has gone away.

CHAPTER 29

AFTER BRENDA LEAVES, SOMEONE ELSE arrives. It's Granny. At least, that's what Theo and Iris and Esme call her. She visits us sometimes.

"Hi, Mom." Will leans over and kisses her on the cheek. She hugs both me and Will and kisses me on my forehead.

"What's wrong with Buddy? He doesn't look too good."

My eyes are so heavy I can hardly keep them open.

"Rough morning. Beyond rough. Buddy here had a total melt-down. Never seen it before like this. Gabby took a toy from him and he completely over-reacted, and the caseworker said he was spoiled, and maybe he is, and Maxine got really mad and snapped at her, and god only knows what's going to happen next. Maybe the caseworker is right. Maybe he is spoiled."

"Or maybe he's just being a baby. Let me have him." Granny takes me in her arms.

I don't really care whose arms hold me because I pulled my disappearing trick.

We go back inside where Gabby is sitting on the ground and taking off the socks Maxine just put on her.

"Mom, are you sure you can handle this? Gabby's a handful, and Buddy's out of sorts. I feel bad leaving them," Will says.

"What do you mean, can I handle it? You and your brothers gave me a run for my money when you were kids, and I'm no worse for the wear."

"You're a better woman than I am. Because it's only been a week, and I feel way worse for the wear!" Maxine calls out as she scoops up a running Gabby and sets her in her lap. Gabby squirms while Maxine wrestles socks onto her feet for the second time.

"NO!" Gabby cries. She pulls the socks off again and throws them down. Maxine looks completely frazzled and there's water on her cheeks again.

"I don't feel right leaving, either," Maxine says to Granny. "It's too much. For Buddy. For Gabby. For you. Gabby hasn't gotten settled yet and she needs constant attention. It doesn't feel fair to leave her, not after what she's been through. And Buddy—God only knows what his problem is. He's a mess."

"I know, but this court date is important. I don't want either of us to miss it," Will says. He's starting to look frazzled, too.

"You go. I'll stay. I can't leave these two. Granny, I'm sorry you came over for nothing. I'm just going to stay home with them." Maxine eyes and face are red.

"Here's what we're going to do." Granny looks at Will and points a finger at him. "You go to court." She turns to Maxine and holds me out to her. "You two go back to bed." Then she looks down at Gabby. "And you, Fireball, are coming with me. We're having a Granny Day."

"Mom, are you sure?" Will asks.

"What do you mean? Of course I'm sure." She already has both socks and shoes on Gabby's feet.

"Do you think it's okay if I don't go to court?" Maxine asks Will.

"Probably a good idea *not* to go. You might cuss out the judge." Will smiles for the first time since Gabby's caseworker Brenda arrived.

"That is not funny," Maxine says.

"It kinda is," he replies. "I can't believe you said that to Brenda. I about fell over."

"She deserved it," Maxine replies. For the first time, she smiles, too.

"That'll make a great story. Someday. As long as she doesn't hold it against us."

"She probably will. I don't trust her as far as I can throw her!" Maxine turns to Granny. "You sure about this?"

"I already said I was!"

"Well then, I'm going to put Buddy down and then I'm going to put myself down. Thank you so much. You are a lifesaver."

"No problem. We're going to have a great day. Don't you worry about a thing." Gabby is pulling on Granny's hand and headed toward the door.

"I'll walk out with you. So much for a shower! I guess it'll have to wait until I get home," Will says as he grabs his keys. He turns and kisses Maxine and me.

Within minutes, I'm in my crib and sound asleep, disappeared for real.

CHAPTER 30

"Buddddy … Buddddy Boyyyy … wake up, sleepy head."

My eyes flutter for a little bit, and then I lift my head up. It's Esme.

"You slept all day, silly boy. You must've been tired," Esme says. She reaches into my crib and pulls me close to her body. I lay my head on her shoulder as she carries me to the kitchen. She gives me to Maxine, who kisses me and rubs her hand over the top of my head.

I'm in my high chair after a quick diaper change. I like when we are all sitting together. I look from one face to another while I pick up the food on my tray. Something feels different. I can just tell.

There's not as much talking as usual. I've gotten used to lots of talking. Everybody talks to each other and they talk to me, even if I don't talk back. Sometimes, they even talk at the same time. When that happens, I never know for sure who will talk the longest. Usually it's Esme.

Gabby tries to shovel food into her mouth, but Will sits next to her and slows her down.

"So, who has homework tonight?" Maxine asks.

"Not me," Esme and Theo say at the same time.

"I do. Just math," Iris says.

"How long is it going to take? You probably should have done it after school, because you have basketball practice tonight," Maxine tells her.

"It won't take me long. Who's taking me to practice?"

"I am. Your dad needs to catch up on his sleep."

"Can I go, too?" Theo asks.

"And me?" says Esme.

"Of course."

"If you want to take Buddy, I'll put Gabby to bed early while you're gone. I think she's about to fall asleep," Will says.

I look over at Gabby. It's true. She's not shoveling food in her mouth anymore and she's not squirming to get out of her seat.

"I think Granny wore her out today," Maxine says. "Thank God for your mother!"

"What did they do all day?" Iris asks.

"They went to the park then had lunch then played some more. Gabby will sleep good tonight."

I throw my sippy cup on the floor just because I feel like it. "Uh-oh," I say.

"We told you, Dad! Buddy said his first word today!"

"He sure did. You gonna say it again? Uh-oh." Will has a big smile on his face. I smile back.

"Uh-oh," I say again. They all clap and make a lot of noise. Gabby looks up.

"Uh-oh," she says. We start taking turns like we do at night when we wait for sleep. Everyone is giggling. I love when that happens.

"They seem to be speaking the same language," Maxine says.

"Maybe Gabby taught him that," Theo says.

"Probably. It's a good word for these two. They've definitely both had plenty of 'uh-ohs' in their lives." Will looks tired.

"Wasn't there court today? On Buddy's case?" Theo asks.

"Yes," Will responds.

"Well, what happened? Anything?"

There's a long pause. "Not a whole lot. Looks like Buddy won't be going back to his mom. He might start visiting with his dad, though. Still not sure, since the dad didn't come to court today."

"I thought nobody knew who Buddy's dad was," Theo says. There's another long pause.

"Technically, that's true," Maxine says. "But … Buddy's mom had a boyfriend when Buddy was born, so the court considers him like a dad, too."

"I thought Buddy's mom was in jail," Theo says next. Every time he says something, silence hangs in the air while Theo looks at Maxine, Maxine looks at Will, and Esme and Iris look at all of them. I'm just gnawing on a piece of bread crust, wondering what will happen next.

"She is," Will says.

"She and her boyfriend are in jail?" Esme asks.

"No, honey. Just Buddy's mom," Maxine says. She's looking at Will again.

"But they're still boyfriend and girlfriend?"

"I don't think so," Maxine says. "We don't really need to worry about that, though."

"But why does the boyfriend get to be like Buddy's dad when he's not Buddy's dad?"

"Well, that's a good question. I don't think we can answer that one," Will says.

"Is Buddy going to go live with him?" Iris asks.

"I'm not sure what will happen," Will says.

"Oh, I forgot to ask you." Maxine is looking at Will. "Did you ever meet Buddy's GAL? Who is it? Why haven't we even met her yet? I mean, I'm assuming it's a girl. Most are."

"You are wrong. It is a guy. Name's Justin Miller. And no, I didn't meet him because he didn't show up."

"You mean he missed court?" Maxine sounds shocked. "What the heck?"

"He called in after we waited for about twenty minutes. Said he had the date wrong. It didn't matter much, though. It's not like he had anything to add."

"How long is Buddy going to be here?" Iris asks.

"I don't know, honey. At least the next few months, probably longer," Will tells her.

"I hope he stays forever," Esme says.

"You always want every foster kid to stay forever," Iris responds. "Maybe he will, maybe he won't."

"Who knows? Let's finish up and get to the rec center." Maxine stands and starts clearing the table because no one is eating anymore.

Not even Gabby.

The kids all scatter, but I stay in my high chair. When the table is cleared and the dishes are gone, Maxine wipes my face and hands—which I hate—and then picks me up.

Will and Gabby stay behind while the rest of us pile into the van. Theo helps me with the straps on my car seat and then hands me X. I never go in the van unless I have her with me.

I love to ride in the van with all the kids, but this time, I just look out the window and watch things pass by instead of turning my head toward whoever is talking.

Everybody bounces out of the van and runs ahead. Maxine lifts me out of my seat. She takes X from my hands and sets her down where I was sitting.

"Let's leave X here. We don't want her to get lost. Give her a kiss."

I lean forward and put my lips on X. I give kisses now. But only when I want to.

We walk in the doors to the rec center. I love this place!

There are all kinds of people at the rec center and they do lots of different things. We head toward the gym, where Iris is tossing a ball with another girl. Theo and Esme are playing ball on the other side.

"Hey Buddy Wuddy, whassup?" It's one of Theo's friends. Everybody has lots of friends here. This one holds his hand out high and I put my own against it, and then he keeps walking. He doesn't seem to be waiting for me to say anything and that's fine with me.

Maxine sets me down on the ground and I stand with both feet. I can walk if someone holds my hand. I hold onto Maxine's fingers.

"Hey, Maxine. How's it going?" a lady asks. I have seen her lots of times before. She's Maxine's friend.

"Okay," Maxine says. "No, wait. That's a lie. This day has sucked. It started with an unexpected home visit from Gabby's caseworker and went downhill from there. Thank God for Will's mom. She was going to watch Buddy and Gabby while Will and I went to court for Buddy's hearing, but the morning was so crazy that I ended up staying home with Buddy and sleeping. Will's mom took Gabby out, and Will went to court alone."

"How was court?" she asks.

"Here's what I don't get. Will and I go through this three-ring circus to make sure we are there. Will took off work, his mom was going to stay with the kids, we had it all figured out. Then Gabby's worker shows up, all hell breaks loose, Will goes to court, and then Buddy's GAL doesn't even show up."

"You're kidding! She just didn't come?"

"It's a he, and no. Who knows why? But seriously, how do you just not show up for court when it's your job? Maybe I wouldn't be so crabby about it if I'd even met the guy. He's never been to our home, and Buddy's been with us for over four months."

"Yeah, that's pretty bad."

"Uh-oh," I say. Their eyes are on me. I smile and say it again.

"Buddy, are you talking now?" the friend asks as she bends down and we are face to face. She's happy. Maxine scoops me up.

"He sure is. Just started this morning!" Maxine's smile stretches all the way across her face. "In the midst of all the chaos!"

"Like when the caseworker knocked on the door?" They both laugh.

"Actually, before that." There's a long pause. "I do have to say … the kids were so excited when that baby said 'uh-oh.' We all were. It was one of those moments that make the rest of this crazy fostering stuff worth it."

They both look at me and I smile again before I start to wiggle. I want to get down, so Maxine sets me on the ground. I hold onto her fingers again.

A gaggle of little girls is running by, but eventually, they circle back. I know all their faces. I've seen them here before.

"Hi, Buddy. Wanna play?" One bends down and is right in my face. I smile at her. She holds out a little ball and I reach for it. I let go of Maxine's fingers. Both of my hands are good now and I can hold the ball by myself.

"Here Buddy, throw it back!" she says. I just look at her.

"Can I take him, Mrs. Jackson?" a little girl asks.

"You can play with him. But you have to stay right here."

The girl sits down on the ground in front of me and holds her hands out for the ball so I give it to her.

"You wanna sit down with me?" she asks. She pats the ground and holds out her hand. I don't move, so she sets the ball down on the ground.

I bend over, pick it up and then fall on my bottom.

"Uh-oh," I say. The girl and her friends giggle. I smile at them and say it again. Then I push the ball across the ground.

We do this for a little while, and then we walk around some while I hold the girl's hand. No matter where we are, I can always see Maxine.

Eventually, we all climb back into the car and head home. The house is quiet.

"We're hooooome!" Theo calls out in a loud voice. He always does that whenever he walks in the door.

"Theo, *shhhh!* Your dad and Gabby might be sleeping."

Esme runs down the hall and pops her head into the bedrooms.

"Yep, they're sleeping!" she whispers to us after she runs back.

"It's about that time. Girls, you both need showers. Theo, here, can you take Buddy and get him ready for bed? I changed him right before we left the gym, so he just needs jammies. Be careful not to wake Gabby."

"Let's go, Buds," Theo says as he reaches out for me. We walk down the hallway toward my room and Theo very quietly opens the door. We step inside. He walks over to Gabby's crib and looks down at her sleeping.

"She's out like a light," he whispers. With his free hand, he kisses his fingers and presses them lightly on her head. "Do you wanna give her kisses, too?" He holds up his fingers and I put my lips against them then he touches her head for the second time.

"Good boy. So, jammies. Let's see here …" He digs through my dresser drawer. "We got trains, we got dinosaurs, we got baseballs … what're we going for?" I just smile at him.

"Let's do trains," he says as he pulls out a one-piece sleeper.

We go back into the living room, where he lays me down on the floor. I play with a book while he pulls up the zipper.

"Wanna read this one?" he asks. He scoops me up and we sit on the couch. I like to sit on his lap. Maxine walks by and kisses Theo on the head.

"Thanks for your help. You're my good boy," she says.

"As opposed to your bad boy?" Theo asks.

"Ha. I don't have any bad boys. Just good ones." She kisses me on the head, too.

"He slept a long time today. Do you think he'll be ready to go to bed soon?"

"I think so. He exhausted himself this morning with a fit unlike I've ever seen before. Besides, usually the gym wears him out."

"Poor Buddy. Don't worry. Those days happen to everybody," Theo says as he opens the book and begins to read. I sit very still and listen to his voice. I love how it changes when he says different words. When he is finished, he stands up and hands me to Maxine.

I rest my head on her shoulder as soon as I'm in her arms.

I don't know what will happen next.

I just hope Something Next never comes.

CHAPTER 31

IT'S MY BIRTHDAY TODAY. AT least, that's what everyone keeps saying. I am two years old and I have lots of new words.

I have new tricks, too. My favorite trick is running like Gabby does, but I'm not as fast.

Gabby runs to the couch, scampers up onto it, and looks out the window.

"Granny, Granny, Granny," she yells. At the sound of Granny's name, I come running, too. Granny walks inside, carrying lots of stuff in her arms.

"Well, if it isn't the birthday boy and an angel," she says. I throw my arms around her leg and Gabby hugs her other one. She bends down and kisses both of us.

"Hi, Granny!" Iris says. "I didn't know you were bringing balloons."

"What's a birthday party without balloons?" She starts handing things over to Iris, and eventually all of her hands are free. "Where is everyone?"

"Mom and Esme are in the kitchen. Dad had to go to the grocery. He's gone like a million times today already. He keeps forgetting stuff. Theo is around here somewhere. Probably in the kitchen. Who knows?"

"Ma ma ma ma ma ma," I tell her as I point to the kitchen. "Come."

"Is that where she is?" Granny bends down to look me in the eye. I nod and walk toward the kitchen with her close behind.

"What can I do to help?" Granny asks.

"I have vegetables that still need to be cut up. Do you mind?" Before Granny says anything, Mom hands her a bag. There's lots of colors inside.

"Why bother?" Theo says as he sticks his hand in a bag of potato chips. "Vegetables always go beggin' at a party anyway."

"It makes me feel better," Mom says. "Get out of those." She takes the bag from Theo and puts it away.

"Granny, come look at Buddy's cake. It's a train. We made it!" Granny scoops me up and walks over to the counter.

"Choo choo," I say. I stick my finger out to touch it but Granny pulls me back.

"Sorry, Buddy Boy, no fingers in the cake. At least, not yet."

"Here, have a chip." Theo holds out his hand. I grab a chip from it and stuff it into my mouth.

"Look, Mom, Granny brought balloons." Iris is holding a string with a bunch of big red and blue circles that are high in the air. I've never seen anything like them before. I'm not sure I like them. They kind of scare me.

"Can I have one?" Gabby asks. Iris pulls one out from the bunch and hands it to her. Gabby laughs and jumps up and down. She takes off running with the balloon flying behind her.

"Gabby, slow down!" Mom reaches out an arm to stop Gabby as she races by. She bends down and looks into her eyes. "Be careful, sweetie. You have to watch where you're going."

Gabby nods her head and looks up at her balloon. As soon as Mom turns away, Gabby is running again, faster and faster until she trips over a toy on the floor. She lets go and the balloon floats up, up in the air.

POP! The big balloon is gone and the string falls to the floor.

I start screaming and I can't stop. My heart is bouncing all around inside my body and my arms and legs are tingling.

"Shhh, it's okay, Buddy. It's just a loud noise," Granny says. I don't listen to her though. I just scream and scream and scream, even though my throat feels on fire. There's screaming on my insides, too. I can't make it stop. Nothing can make it stop. Granny passes me to Mom.

"It's alright, sweet boy. Did that big noise scare you? I bet it did." Mom's voice is soothing as she holds me close. I bury my head in her chest. My muffled screams continue as my tears fall onto her shirt in puddles. My fist winds around the sleeve of her shirt and I clench it tightly while she holds me and sways back and forth.

"There's nothing to be afraid of. I got you. It was just a loud noise." Her voice is low and soft. I slowly stop screaming so I can hear her. The sound helps my bouncing heart settle down.

"Here, Buddy. I found X. You want her?" I turn my head just a little bit and with one eye, I see Esme holding X. I untangle my fingers and reach out. I tuck her under my arm and lay my head back down.

I'm not screaming anymore and the screaming on my insides has quieted down, too. Granny is sitting with Gabby on her lap. Gabby's not crying though. She never cries. She's never scared of anything.

There's a knock on the door. It creaks open, but I don't even look up. I just lay quietly with my head resting on Mom's chest.

"Hi, Aunt Anita!" Esme and Iris call out.

"Hey girls, how's it going?"

"Well," Esme begins, "it was going pretty good until Gabby was running and let go of a balloon that Granny brought and it popped on a lightbulb on the ceiling and made a loud noise and scared Buddy really bad. Do you want to see his cake?"

"Sure. Maxine, what else needs to be done in the kitchen?"

"If you can start putting the food out, that would be great. The kids can help. I need to sit here with Buddy for a little bit. Will should be home in a minute. He ran out to get ice."

The front door opens and closes a bunch more times and the room fills with lots of different voices. Dad walks through the door and heads straight to the kitchen.

"Hey Buddy, wanna go outside on the swing set?" A girl the size of Theo has Gabby in her arms. She holds out a hand to me.

I look out the window and see kids swinging. Some are playing ball and some are just running around. Esme is laughing. I can't hear it, but I can see her face. She looks happy and I'm sure she's making noise.

I'm not sure what to do. It's nice to sit in Mom's lap, to have her all to myself, even though she's talking to someone and not to me. My insides are all settled down now.

146

"Come on, Buddy, let's have some fun." I don't know where Theo came from, but here he is, standing in front of me with his arms outstretched. I look at Mom, then up at Theo, then at Mom again. She's still talking to someone. I guess she's done talking to me. I hold X by her ear and lift my arms.

"Make way for the birthday boy," Theo says as we move between the people who are standing around talking. He straps me into a swing and I start moving back and forth, back and forth. I love the way the air feels on my scrunched-up face so I stick my tongue out, too. Just for fun.

Theo and the girl start laughing. Then Gabby starts laughing, so I do, too.

All of me feels better, including my insides.

My train cake has two candles on it. All the people are looking at me and singing. I have no idea why. I look from one face to another and all of them are smiling—well, except for Esme. I don't know why she's not smiling. She smiles more than anybody I know.

"Blow 'em out, Buddy, like this," Dad says as his lips turn into a circle and air comes out of his mouth. He is holding me in his big, strong arms and bending down just a tiny bit toward the train cake on the table. I try to do what he does, but nothing happens, even though I *know* how to blow. I blow kisses. And bubbles, because Iris taught me how to do that a long time ago.

I try some more and still nothing happens until Dad leans his face next to mine and blows, too. Everyone claps, even me.

I make a mess with my train cake, or at least the piece Mom puts on my high chair tray. I squish the soft icing between my fingers then shove them into my mouth. I'm in heaven. I love how it tastes. I love to play with it, too, so I do both at the same time. I'm getting big and I can do more than one thing at a time now. I know. New trick!

"Here's your drink, Buddy," Mom says as she hands me a sippy cup. It's slippery in my hands, but I get it up to my mouth anyway and take a drink.

"Is he still on that nasty Pediasure?" Aunt Anita asks.

"Nope!" Mom has a big smile on her face. "He's gotten so big and healthy he doesn't need it anymore."

"You must be really happy about that!"

"Not as happy as Buddy. Right, Buds?" Mom turns to look at me and she and Anita both laugh.

"You are a mess!" Aunt Anita says.

"Trust me, I'll take this kind of mess any day."

Eventually, the house is quiet again and all the people have gone away.

"Ugh, why do I feel like I'm going to have a birthday party hangover in the morning?" Mom asks as she flops on the couch.

"Probably because you will. Man, I always forget how much work parties are until we have one," Dad says. "It was worth it, though. Buddy seemed happy enough. I was a little worried when he had a meltdown right before everybody got here."

"I kind of was too, but he seems to bounce back faster and faster from those episodes. It used to take him forever."

I listen to them talk as I sit quietly in Esme's lap. She's quiet, too. That almost never happens. Her chin is resting on my head and I can feel her breathe deeply.

"I love how soft his hair is and how good it smells after his bath," she says with her nose in my hair. "I could sit here forever and hold him when he's cuddly like this."

"He is tired, that's for sure. Busy day for him. For all of us," Dad says.

"You seem tired, too." Mom looks over at Esme. "You've been pretty quiet." Immediately, there's water in Esme's eyes.

"Honey, what's wrong?"

"It's just … I can't help but think … I mean, I wonder what his birthday was like last year? Do you think anybody was happy when he turned one?"

"I don't know, sweetheart. That's a tough question."

"I mean, what if nobody cared? That makes me so sad." Water is flowing down her face. She brushes it aside with the back of her hand.

"Yeah, it's a sad thing to think about. I thought about that, too."

"Doesn't it make you sad?"

"Well, for a minute. It is sad. But then I look at Buddy. Do you think he's sad?"

Esme looks down at me. I reach up and pat her face. She grabs my hand and kisses it, so I blow a kiss to her. She smiles, and I do, too.

"No, he doesn't look sad. Not right now, anyway."

"There are things from his past that are really sad, but there are things today that are happy. That's most important."

"I guess. It's just hard sometimes to think about it."

"That's because you love him so much. And loving him is the most important thing we can do, especially since his life was sad before he got here."

"When he came, I kind of tried not to love him, because it is so hard to say good-bye. But it was impossible. I couldn't not love him."

"It's hard to love someone, no doubt about that. It's much harder not to, though. Imagine if nobody loved Buddy. That would be horrible. That's the saddest thing I can think of happening, even sadder than if nobody was happy on his first birthday."

No one says anything for a long time.

"I guess so. But I hope we never have to say good-bye to him. Or to Gabby. I love them both so much."

"I know you do. And I love that about you. Whatever happens, it's going to be okay."

Their words are soft and warm. They swirl around the room and eventually land on me like a comfy blanket as my eyes slowly close and they settle inside of me.

I want to stay here forever.

CHAPTER 32

"Awake!" I call out for the third time. No one has come for me yet, but I don't worry, because I know someone will. Someone always comes now.

I'm standing in my crib, holding onto the rails and waiting. What is taking them so long?

My bedroom door swings open.

"Okay, big boy, I hear you," Mom says as she reaches in to fetch me and kisses me on my forehead, but I don't think she's happy. I can even feel it in her arms. They aren't bad arms, or bad hands, but they feel … weird.

She carries me into the living room where a lady is sitting on the couch across from Dad. She looks up from a pad of paper on her lap. Gabby is on the swing outside and Iris is pushing her.

"Oh yes, now I remember. This is your other foster baby," the lady says. "The one who was crying and carrying on last time I was here."

"Brenda, his name is Buddy," Mom says.

"Who did you say his caseworker was?"

"Stephanie Hawkins," Dad says. "Now, back to Gabby. So you say there's a great-grandmother who lives out of state and wants placement. How likely is it that Gabby would move there?"

"It's possible. We always try to place with relatives whenever we can."

There's a long pause. Mom and Dad are looking at each other, as if they're trying to talk to each other not using words. Brenda is looking at them. I'm looking at everybody. Something is going on. I can feel it.

"Can we just be really honest with you?" Dad finally says.

"Of course," Brenda says.

"We're concerned about Gabby going with her great-grandmother. Not because we don't think kids shouldn't be with family, but because Gabby is a handful. She's a busy, busy girl and on the move constantly. I can't imagine how an elderly person will physically keep up with her. How old is the great-grandmother?"

"She's seventy-two, not that it matters. We can't discriminate against her based on age. Just can't do that. Family is family."

"It doesn't make a whole lot of sense that you can't consider her age. I mean, when this lady turns eighty, Gabby won't even be ten years old. Mathematically, how is this a good idea?"

"We're not talking about ten years from now. We're talking about today. And today, there's a relative who wants her."

There's another long pause. I can tell no one is happy, and Mom's arms don't feel any better.

"Our other concern is that this is her mom's paternal grandmother. From what you said before, Gabby's mom and her mom's dad, Gabby's grandfather, were in the system until they were eighteen. So, if this lady, for whatever reason, didn't raise her son *or* her granddaughter, why would the system give her great-granddaughter to her to raise? It just makes no sense to us."

"I can't really speak to those details. All I can say is, the court makes this decision, not me."

"But the court takes your opinion into consideration, doesn't it?"

"It does. But it also listens to the GAL."

"Speaking of the GAL, no one has contacted us. Do you know who it is? Isn't he or she supposed to make a visit by now?"

"Supposed to. I don't know who it is. You can call their office. Someone there can probably tell you."

In a flash, Gabby slides open the screen door and slams it shut.

"Gotta go!" she yells as she flies past us, her feet pounding the floor in a frenzy. The bathroom door slams with a bang so hard it shakes the walls. Mom disappears down the hallway and knocks on the door before opening it.

"Potty-training," Dad says.

"You weren't kidding when you said she was fast!" The lady puts her pad of paper back into her bag and stands when Mom walks into the room holding Gabby's hand.

"Did ya make it?" Dad picks Gabby up and props her on his hip.

"Yep!"

"Did ya wash your hands?"

"Yep!"

"Good job!" He holds out an open hand and she smacks it.

"I'll be in touch," Brenda says before she disappears out the door.

"She's ridiculous! Could she care any less about what happens to Gabby?"

Dad just shakes his head and doesn't say anything.

"And I cannot believe we still haven't heard from a GAL. That's ridiculous, too. I was hoping to hear from someone before I had to chase them down. I'll call that office tomorrow."

She reaches for me and I lift my arms. Her arms still don't feel any better. I knew they wouldn't.

CHAPTER 33

I'M ON MY KNEES ON the floor, moving my big red firetruck back and forth, back and forth and watching the wheels go around and around. For extra fun, I make my *swish swish* noise, but I make it with my mouth and not with my head like I did when I laid in my crib.

My new firetruck is my favorite thing to play with, except for X. Sometimes I put X on top of my firetruck so I can play with both of them at the same time.

Gabby is not my favorite thing to play with, even though she likes to play with me. She's always got her hands in my way. There's only two of them, but they're everywhere!

"Stephanie called today," Mom says to Dad as soon as he walks in the door.

"What'd she have to say?" Dad asks. He leans down and gives me a quick kiss on the top of my head. Gabby runs toward him. Good. Maybe she will stay there and leave me and my truck alone.

"My turn!"

"Well of course it's your turn!" He scoops her up and gives her a kiss on the top of her head while she giggles. He sets her down. She's back. So are her hands, and they are on my truck. Again! I push them off and move my truck back and forth some more while I make my *swish swish* noise.

"Buddy's dad called for visits, so Stephanie set them up. Twice a week, two hours at a time."

"Hmm. Did she say when they were going to start?"

"Next week," Mom says. "Tuesdays and Thursdays from noon to two. I'm glad it's not later in day. At least I can be home in time for the bus."

"I want to go on the bus," Gabby says as she tugs on Mom's pants. Mom bends down to look her in the eye.

"I know you do, sweetie. And you will go to school just like the big kids when you get bigger."

"Are visits going to be down at the center or somewhere like McDonald's?" Dad asks.

"Visitation Center, thank God! I hope Buddy does alright. He hasn't really been away from us at all."

"I'm sure he'll do fine. At least they're supervised. Could be worse. Besides," Dad says, "it'll be good to know where this is going with Buddy. The sooner we know, the sooner he will be settled, either way."

"That's almost exactly what Stephanie said on the phone earlier." Mom reaches down and grabs a book that Gabby is holding up for her to read. Gabby likes books. I do too, but only sometimes.

"Stephanie's on top of things. At least Buddy has that going for him. He's got it better than our girl. Too bad we can't trade Brenda in for another Stephanie."

"Too bad we can't trade Brenda in for no Brenda!"

"Read! Please!" Gabby is tugging on Mom's hand. Dad takes the book in one hand and Gabby's hand in his other.

"Nope, this one's my favorite. I get to read it with you!" Dad settles onto the couch and Gabby climbs in his lap.

No more hands on my truck except mine.

Swish swish swish.

CHAPTER 34

FAST FOOTSTEPS ARE MOVING ALL over the house. I know because I can hear them hit the floor one after the other, quick quick quick. I've heard those fast footsteps before. I'm sure of it. I don't know when, but I don't like the way they make me feel. I reach for X and roll my head back and forth, back and forth and listen for the *swish swish* sound.

After a while, I stand in my crib. Gabby is not in her big girl bed. I don't know where she went.

"Good morning, Buddy Boy," Dad says. He reaches in and pulls me close. I look in his eyes to see what's in there. There's sad. I can tell.

After a quick diaper change, Dad sets me down and I walk down the hall with X tucked under my arm.

There is sad everywhere. I see it in every face. Even Theo has water in his eyes.

Outside, I hear a car door slam. The doorbell rings.

"She's here," Dad says to Mom. Mom doesn't say anything at all. Water is streaming down her face.

Dad opens the door and Brenda walks in.

"Good morning," she says. "How y'all doing?"

"We've been better," Dad says. No one says anything. "Brenda, we expected more notice than one day. You could have given us more time to prepare."

"I don't owe you any notice. As I said before, we have a relative, so Gabby needs to go. That's all there is to it."

"You actually do owe us notice. At least, that's what the law says. But that's beside the point. You owe it to Gabby."

"She'll be fine whether she goes today or next week. These kids get

155

used to moving around."

There's silence again. Nobody moves or says anything. Everything stops except my belly. It drops all the way to my feet and leaves a giant hole in the middle of me. I'm glad I'm in Mom's arms.

"I don't even know how to respond to that," Dad says. There's another long pause.

"We better get going. Don't want to miss our flight. Are these her things?" Brenda points to two duffle bags on the floor next to the door. One is pink and one is green. Gabby likes those colors.

"Almost. Here's one more," Mom says as she hands a shoulder bag to Brenda. "It has her favorite blanket it in, some snacks, a few extras. That's everything. Well, at least everything that can go on a plane."

Gabby is standing beside Theo, holding his hand.

"Gabby, it's time to get your coat on," Mom says, even though there's water in her eyes. "Come here."

"No!" Gabby says.

Dad walks over to her and bends down to look in her eyes.

"Sweetheart, do you remember what we talked about this morning?"

Gabby shakes her head.

"This nice lady here, Ms. Brenda, is going to take you to live with your grandma," Dad explains.

"Great-grandma," Brenda says. I'm not sure, but I think Mom just rolled her watery eyes.

"She might understand grandma more than great-grandma," Will says as he turns toward Brenda and looks at her. He turns back to Gabby, who is still holding Theo's hand. "Your grandma wants you to come and live with her, so today, Ms. Brenda is going to take you to her house."

"I live in *this* house," Gabby says.

"Yes, you've lived in our house for a while and we had lots of fun together, but now it's time for you to live with your grandma. She is so happy you are coming to live with her."

"What about the swing set?" Gabby asks.

"It has to stay here, honey, but I'm sure there are lots of swing sets where your grandma lives. Maybe they are even better than the one we have here."

"Is Theo coming too?" Gabby asks as she looks up at Theo. She's still holding his hand.

"No, sweetheart, Theo is going to stay here with the rest of us."

"Why can't he come?"

Dad and Mom look helplessly at each other. I look from face to face and all I see is sad, sad, sad everywhere.

"Gabby," Theo says as he picks her up in his arms. "I have to stay here, but there will be other kids to play with where you are going."

"We need to get going or we'll miss the plane," Brenda says as she picks up the two duffle bags.

"Okay, guys, time to say good-bye," Dad says. Theo hugs Gabby tight before he puts her down. Iris and Esme hug her, too.

Mom picks her up and holds her for a little time before Dad carries her out the door. Brenda follows behind him, dragging the two duffle bags.

When Dad returns, his eyes are wet, too.

Esme holds out her arms and I move into them. I put my arms around her neck and when I squeeze, the wet from her face lands on mine. There is sad everywhere, and it's inside me, too. I think it is in everybody.

That Running Girl is gone.

CHAPTER 35

"OKAY, BUDDY, DO YOU THINK we got it all? Let's see," Mom says. She is digging through my bag after strapping me in my car seat. "Drink, snacks, diapers, spare clothes, a couple favorite books …,I think that's everything."

"I got X!" I tell her as I hold X high above my head.

"Yes, you do." She slides into the driver's seat and off we go.

I don't know where we are going, but we drive for a long, long time. It's just me and Mom and quiet. There's a lot more quiet since Gabby went away.

The car slows until it stops in front of a tall building. Mom climbs out of her seat and I wait for her to come and open my door, too. When she does, there is another lady standing next to her.

"Hi, Michael!" The lady is looking at me, but I don't know if she's talking to me, because my name is Buddy.

"Everyone calls him Buddy," Mom tells her as she's unbuckling the straps on my car seat. I climb out of my seat and Mom picks me up and puts me on her hip. "Buddy, do you remember we talked about Raymond, the man who wants to meet you? You are going to visit with him and in a little while, I'm going to come back and pick you up."

She's been talking about this Raymond for a while, but I think she's playing a game because she never leaves me with people I've never met before. Never.

"This nice lady here is going to stay with you." She tries to hand me over to this lady I've never seen. I have no idea who she is. I bury my head in Mom's shoulder.

"Come on, Buddy, we're going to have fun," the lady says. "We have all kinds of toys inside and Raymond is waiting for you." She holds her arms out and Mom tries to hand me over. Again.

If this is a game, it's not a fun one, and it makes no sense to me. First, I don't know this lady, and I don't know what her hands are going to be like. I try to stay away from hands I don't know. And why would Mom try to give me to some strange hands? She *never* does that. She always stays with me, and if she's not with me, then I'm with Dad or Granny or Aunt Anita, and they all have good hands.

"No!" I wrap my arms around Mom's neck. I don't think this is a game anymore.

Mom holds me tight and puts her cheek close to my ear.

"It's okay, Buddy. I promise I'll be back. This nice lady is going to take good care of you." She tries again to hand me over to the lady reaching for me.

"NO!" I start kicking my legs, too. Do they not get that I am not going anywhere?

"Hi, Buddy! Wow, look how big you are! I bet you can run all over with those strong legs now."

"Stephanie! I didn't expect to see you here," Mom says. "Buddy, look who it is. It's Stephanie."

I look up and see a face I've seen before. This face comes to my house. She has good hands because they've touched me before, when she's come to see me.

"Where's X, Buddy? He's got to be around here somewhere. I never see you without him."

I look back toward the car where I left X sitting in my seat.

"Seat," I say and point to it. Stephanie reaches in and picks her up.

"X has to come, too. Can't leave her behind. She's going to have so much fun here on her visit. Don't you want to come with us?"

Um … no.

"You and X are both going to have fun on your visit." Mom holds me out to Stephanie, whose arms are waiting for me. Stephanie has X and I know her hands are good hands, but once I am in them, I start to cry.

"Go on, Maxine, we got this. See you in a couple hours," Stephanie says to Mom.

Stephanie and the other lady walk into a building. I'm still in Stephanie's arms and I'm still crying and Stephanie is talking nice words the whole time, even though I'm not listening to her. At least I have X.

"We usually don't see caseworkers over here. I'm here to monitor the visit, you know," the lady says to Stephanie.

"Oh, I know. I just wanted be here to help him get settled, see how it goes."

"This one sure had a hard time leaving his foster mama."

"Well, that's a good thing. It shows he's attached to her and trusts her. The ones that don't cry and go to just anybody … those are the ones we should worry about."

"I'd rather deal with them all day. They're easy," the lady says.

"Easy for you maybe. But this isn't about you. It's about the kids. At least, it should be."

They stop talking. We walk until we reach a room at the end of the hall. I'm not crying anymore.

A man stands up and walks toward us.

"Raymond, good to see you. How are you?" Stephanie reaches out to shake his hand. He takes her hand in his, but he is looking at me. I can tell, even though I don't look up.

"Doing alright," he says.

"Raymond, this is Buddy." Stephanie shifts me in her arms, but I don't move and I don't say anything.

"Hey there, Buddy." Raymond reaches out and touches my back. I freeze, even though his hands don't have sizzle—at least, not yet.

"Why don't we see what kind of toys they have here?" Stephanie asks. She sets me on the ground and I stand. "Raymond, is there anything good in that box?"

Raymond reaches in and pulls out a toy car.

"Buddy, look here." He puts the car on the ground and pushes it toward me, but it doesn't move.

He picks it up and looks at it. "Missing a couple wheels."

I look up at Stephanie, who is holding my hand.

"Well, let's see what's in Buddy's bag." She roots through my bag and pulls out some books. I reach out for one and plop down on the floor. Theo always reads this book to me. It's about a dog. I love this one.

"Listen, I'm going to get out of your way so you two can enjoy your visit. Raymond, I'll call you tomorrow to follow up."

By the time I look up, Stephanie is gone. It's just the lady and Raymond. I wish I could pull my disappearing trick.

Raymond sits down on an old, worn couch and takes out his phone. I sit on the floor with my book and X. I still don't know where I am or why I am here, but at least nothing hurts like it always did before.

"Raymond, this is your time to spend with your son, to get to know him. You can't do that if you are on your phone."

"Oh yeah, right, I'm sorry." He puts his phone in his pocket. "Come here, Buddy, come see your old man."

I think Raymond is talking to me because I heard my name, but I act like I don't hear him. I have X and my book. I'm good right here.

"Buddy! Did you hear me?" His voice is louder. Now I'm sure he's calling me. I still don't move.

"Is he deaf or something?"

"Not that I know of. Let me look at his paperwork." The lady shuffles a bunch of papers in her hand. "It doesn't say anything about that in here."

I can hear just fine. That doesn't mean I *want* to hear. I sit very still and don't move so maybe they will go away. Just when I think I'm disappeared, there's a man with his face close to mine. It must be Raymond. I can't breathe and my heart is pounding. He touches my shoulder and I try to get away as fast as I can, but all I do is fall backward and hit my head on the ground with a great big thud. Ouch.

I don't cry, because crying makes everything hurt worse and hands I don't know come for me.

"Look how tough he is! That's my boy alright." Raymond reaches down and picks me up. "I knew you were tough." I'm still frozen inside except my heart, which is pounding.

"That was a pretty hard fall. Does he have a bump on his head?"

the lady asks.

"Nah, he's fine," Raymond says. He rubs his hand across my head. "Didn't even cry."

I don't cry. I don't do anything, especially look in any eyes, even though I know all their eyes are looking at me. I can feel it.

There's only one thing left to do at a time like this.

I pull my disappearing trick and go to sleep.

CHAPTER 36

I WIGGLE JUST A TINY BIT. My eyelids are heavy and it takes a while for them to open.

"When I picked him up, they said he slept nearly the entire visit and he is still out. I don't know what happened, but apparently he hit his head." It's Mom's voice and I'm in my car seat. Her voice has worry. I can tell. Then there's silence.

"Yeah, so we're on our way now. Can you meet me down there? I'm so stressed out. Trying not to be." There's more silence. She must be talking on her phone. She does that sometimes.

"Okay, I'll meet you in the ER. I think he's waking up." She half-turns her head to look at me and we lock eyes, but hardly at all because she turns her head back around.

"Buddy, sweet baby, are you okay? I wish I could have been with you." I rub X's paw back and forth between my finger and thumb, but I don't do anything or say anything else.

The car stops and Mom pulls me out of my seat. We head through big glass doors. I have been here before. I know I have. Suddenly my heart is pounding again.

"Hey, Buddy, I heard you took a knock on the head." It's Dad. I reach my arms out for him. He turns to Mom. "How hard was it?"

"I don't know. The person who brought him out just said he fell and hit his head during the visit."

"That's all she said? Why didn't she tell you more?"

"Because she didn't know. She wasn't there. She said she only supervised the second half of the visit."

"Did you ask Raymond?"

"No. They don't let you talk to or see the parents anymore before or after visits. It's a new policy," Mom says.

"Let me see you, Buddy Boy." Dad stares into my eyes. I think he's looking for something, but I don't know what it is. "Are you hungry?"

I nod and Mom hands me a cracker. I'm starving! I reach out for my sippy cup with my other hand.

"Michael Wilson," a loud voice calls out and we follow a man down the hall into a small white room. Everything is white.

I don't like white. I don't like this. I don't like this place.

"So, this is Michael Wilson?" the man asks as his fingers move across a small computer.

"Yes, but his nickname is Buddy."

"And you're his parents?"

"Foster parents."

"Oh." He looks up at Mom and Dad. His eyes move from one to the other. I think he's looking for something too, but I don't know what it is. I guess he didn't find it, because he looks back down at his computer. "What brings you here today?"

"Well, Buddy was on a two-hour supervised visit with his father at Children's Services. When I picked him up, the person who brought him out to me told me he had fallen and hit his head, and after that, he slept the entire time," Mom says.

"How far did he fall?"

"I'm really not sure. That was all they could tell me."

"Did he fall off a couch or something?"

"I really don't know."

There's silence. They all just keep looking at each other.

"More cracker." I hold my hand out toward Mom.

"Say please," she says. She always says that when I want something. All the time.

"Please."

She hands one to me. "What do you say?"

"Thank you." I shove it in my mouth.

"You're welcome."

I sit on Mom's lap and munch on my cracker. They're still looking at each other.

"Do you have any concerns about him since you picked him up?" The man with the computer looks confused.

"Not really. Now that he's awake, he seems fine. But when I picked him up, and he was asleep and hard to rouse, I called his caseworker to try and find out exactly what happened at this visit. She didn't know, so she talked to her supervisor, and they told us to bring him in and have him seen, just to be on the safe side."

"Okay, I'm going to get some vitals and the doc will be in shortly."

We've been here forever, me and Mom and Dad, stuck in this tiny white room with no more crackers. My sippy cup is empty, too. I just want to go home. I think Mom and Dad do, too.

There's a knock on the door and a White Coat comes in.

"Hi, folks, my name is Dr. Brinn. Sorry for the delay. What brings you here today?"

Haven't we already gone through this?

"This is our foster son, Buddy. He fell and hit his head today while he was on a supervised visit with his dad, but we don't have any other details. He apparently slept most of the visit and I had a hard time getting him awake when I picked him up, so his caseworker and supervisor told me to have him seen."

"Let's get him up on the table here so I can take a look."

Dad tries to set me down, but the paper on the table makes noise and I don't like it. I cling to him instead.

"It's okay Buddy, you sit and I'll stay right here," Dad says. "I'm not going anywhere."

"No!"

"You can hold him, that's fine. I just need to get a good look."

I stay in Dad's arms and White Coat comes closer. He pulls out a little light and flashes it in my eyes. I shut them really fast because I don't know his face or his eyes and I don't want to see them.

"Buddy, can you open your eyes and let me take a peek?"

165

I bury my head in Dad's shoulder and I pretend there is no White Coat.

At least I have X.

"Buddy, come on now. Open your eyes. It's not going to hurt. I promise." Dad shifts and juggles me, trying to pull my face from his shirt.

I clutch X under my arm with my eyes tight shut and I'm not going to open them because first, they can't make me, and second, I don't want to. They can make me go with strange people I've never seen before and they can leave me but they can't make me open my eyes. So I won't.

"I see you have a little friend with you, Buddy. Who's this little pup?"

I don't answer.

"That's X," Mom says. "X has been with Buddy for a long time, longer than we have."

"Well then, maybe X can tell me what's going on with Buddy. Hello, X."

I listen real close. Nobody has ever talked to X before.

"X, let's have a look in your eyes. Hold real still." I'm still clutching X under my arm, but White Coat can see her face.

"Oh wow, look at that! Those big brown eyes are perfect, just perfect. Very healthy. Does Buddy have the same color eyes as you do?"

White Coat waits for X to answer, but of course, X doesn't answer because she doesn't talk.

"Oh, you don't know? Do you think he'll let me look?" White Coat keeps talking to X. His voice is nice, and I like that he talks to X. I open my eyes to take a closer look at him.

"Would you look at that? Buddy and X *do* have the same color eyes. I wonder if Buddy's eyes look as good as X's eyes look? What do you think, Buddy? Should we take a look and see?" His hand is moving around the top of my head but I don't mind because I'm in Dad's arms and I still have X. White Coat's hands don't have sizzle. I can tell.

He moves a light slowly across my face, but it doesn't hurt.

"His eyes are just as perfect as X's eyes. Very healthy. Wow, two sets of perfect eyes. It's a good day!"

I don't look at White Coat, but his voice is happy and his hands still don't have sizzle. And he talks to X, so I don't mind when he does more things like look in my ears while he asks Mom and Dad lots of questions about what I eat and how I sleep, but I stopped listening because I'm tired and I don't really care.

Finally, Dad hands me over to Mom, who hands me a new sippy cup. I take it from her.

"I don't see any reason for concern," White Coat says. "Just watch him closely over the next couple of days. If he sleeps a lot, vomits, or experiences significant changes in speech or if he complains about pain, bring him right in. Otherwise, call your pediatrician if you have other concerns."

"In a couple more days, it'll be time for another supervised visit with his father. Hopefully, that one won't end like this one," Mom says.

"I'm glad he's okay," Dad says. "Thank you, Dr. Brinn."

"My pleasure. You all take good care. Bye, Buddy." White Coat leaves the room.

It's dark by the time we go outside. I fall asleep as soon as the car starts to move.

After dinner and jammies, I sit with Theo, who reads me my dog book. It's my favorite. My lip starts to quiver.

"Buddy, what's wrong?"

With that, tears fall out of my eyes and I cry and cry and cry. Theo picks me up and carries me to Mom. She reaches her arms out.

"Oh Buddy, what happened?" I'm crying so hard, I can hardly breath.

"Nothing. He just started crying. I have no idea why," Theo says.

"Shh, it's alright, Buddy Boy," Mom whispers while she holds me close and I cry and cry and cry. After forever, I start to catch my breath as she sways with me in her arms.

I feel better, but only a tiny bit. Something Next came today, and

I wasn't ready for it.
  I didn't like it.

CHAPTER 37

SOMETHING NEXT COMES MORE TIMES. I don't like to come and see Raymond, but I'm getting used to it. His hands don't have sizzle, but he doesn't talk to me much, which is my favorite thing in the whole world. Sometimes he reads books to me, but only if the lady tells him to. Sometimes I just sleep, because there's nothing better to do. The lady who sits with us doesn't talk much, either. When it's time to leave, she tells us to say good-bye and Raymond hugs me.

I rub my eye with one hand and hold the lady's hand with the other while we walk down the hall.

"Sleepy again today?" Mom asks when I hold my arms out to her and she picks me up. I nod my head and put it on her shoulder.

"He had a good visit," the lady says as she hands Mom my bag with all my stuff in it.

"Thanks. We'll see you next week," Mom says.

I climb into my car seat with heavy eyes.

"Don't do it, Buddy! Don't all asleep!" Mom starts singing. She's very loud. My eyes pop open wide.

"Look, Buddy! I see a FedEx truck. Do you see it? You love FedEx trucks."

I sit up as tall as I can in my seat and look out the window. I see it!

"X!" I yell as I point out the window. Then I lift X up so she can see, too.

"Let's keep looking. I bet we can find another one."

X and I keep looking out the window and Mom keeps singing and talking all the way home.

"Good job, you made it! Let's get you changed and ready for a nap."

Before I can blink, I'm sound asleep.

My room is very quiet now because there is no one in the other crib. Sometimes, I lay in my crib and say "uh-oh" like I did before. I wait to see if anyone will say it too, like Gabby did, but nobody does, and that's fine with me because I like it quiet.

It's more quiet at the dinner table, too.

"Iris, will you put some peas on Buddy's tray?" Mom asks as she passes Esme a bowl. The stuff in it is green.

"Sure, Mom. Here you go, Buddy." Iris puts a scoop of food on my tray. "It's your favorite."

Peas are *not* my favorite. I scrunch my nose and shake my head. Esme giggles. Maybe tonight won't be quiet at dinner.

"Come on, Buddy, just try one bite."

"No! Yuck!" I shake my head some more, just in case they missed it the first time. I reach for my sippy cup and take a big drink of milk.

"He's not going to eat those, Mom. He hates peas," Theo says. At least Theo knows I'm not going to eat that green stuff. I don't know why Mom won't listen to him.

"That doesn't mean we're going to stop offering them. I read somewhere that you have to offer kids the same food twenty times, even if they don't like it, because they might change their mind." She holds a spoon up to me again.

"No no no no no!" I hit the spoon out of her hand and the peas go flying.

"Buddy, no. No hitting. You know better than that," Mom says. Her face is mad, but I don't care.

"Somebody has a temper today," Iris says.

"It's visit day. No surprise here," Mom says as she cuts up chicken and puts it on my tray.

"Nobody should have to eat peas on visit day, Mom," Theo says. "Here, Buddy, have some chicken. It's yummy." I look down at my tray, pick up a piece of chicken, and throw it on the floor.

"NO!" My face is mad now, too. All of me is mad, so I throw my sippy cup across the room, too.

"That's enough!" Dad says. Now his face is mad. I don't care, and I don't know what else to do, so I just start screaming. And I scream and scream and scream and I might never stop.

Dad's hands reach for me, but I'm not even scared, because they've never had sizzle. He takes me to the bathroom and washes my hands and face, which just makes me scream louder, because I hate that.

"Buddy, I know you're mad. I know this is hard. I'm sorry. But you can't hit and throw things."

I just keep screaming. He's holding me in his arms, but I just want down, so I start kicking, too.

"Okay, looks like you need to take a time out." He carries me to my crib and puts me down. I cling to the sides and scream as loud as I can while he walks away.

I don't know how long I've been screaming when Mom pokes her head in the doorway. I reach my arms out to her, even though I'm screaming. She comes to pick me up. I take big breaths and hiccup while she rubs my back.

"Oh, Buddy Boy, it's a hard day, I know. You're alright, though." She keeps talking quietly and rubbing my back, and it makes my insides feel better.

"X," I say, so she reaches for my toy dog and hands her to me. I hold her tight.

"Are you ready to rejoin the family?"

I nod my head. Mom carries me and X back out to the living room.

"Hey Buddy Wuddy, big boy! You're back." Esme says as she holds her arms out for me. I don't reach out to her though. Instead, I put my head on Mom's shoulder.

It is a hard day.

All the big kids are in bed and I get Mom and Dad all to myself. I love these nights. They almost never come and when they do, they are my favorite.

"What do you want to watch?" Dad asks as he pushes buttons on the TV remote. I don't try to push the buttons, though. I only do that to Theo and Iris and Esme. I just sit cuddled up in Dad's lap and stay quiet.

"Finally!" Mom plops down on the couch next to Dad. "A chance to talk to you about my conversation with Stephanie. She called today."

"About Buddy's visits?"

"No. Well, yes. She mentioned that it looks like they'll be starting overnights soon. She also asked if we'd be willing to take another placement."

There's a long pause.

"We told our worker we needed a break after Gabby. Didn't she know that?"

"Actually, I don't think she *did* know that. She was asking about another case of hers. It's a four-year-old boy. His name is Raphael. He's on his second foster home already and Stephanie wants to get him out of the one he's in."

"What's wrong with the one he's in?" Dad asks.

"He's with a single, older woman who works full-time during the day *and* takes night classes. He's bouncing between two different child care centers, and it's too much."

"That's ridiculous. Why in the hell would they put him with someone who was never home?"

"I asked Stephanie the same thing. I left out the cuss word, though," Mom says.

"That's a first." There's another pause. "How can people get licensed to foster when they have no time to parent?"

"You know how it is. A worker puts in a request for a foster home and gets a name and address. That's how it goes. Stephanie didn't know the details before she placed him. Besides, it's not like she had a choice. There are always too many kids and not enough foster homes. Sometimes, they even have kids sleeping on cots at the office because there is literally nowhere for them to go."

"I don't know, Maxine. Sometimes I think we're crazy for fostering at all. I mean, we're doing our part, raising three good kids, and we have Buddy. For now. Maybe that's enough. We can't save every kid."

"I know. We don't have to save every kid. We are just being asked to consider taking care of Raphael."

"Do you ever wish we could just quit? Live in our bubble and ignore the fact that these kids exist?" he asks.

"Of course I do. Like, at least once a week! But that's useless, because we do know they exist. We can't un-know that."

There's a long pause while Mom looks at Dad and Dad looks away and I look from one to the other. I think they forget I'm sitting here, even though I'm on Dad's lap. They both look sad.

"Gabby hit you hard, didn't she?" Mom asks. It's quiet for a long time.

"I guess she did." Dad lets out a big, long sigh. He looks up at Mom. "I couldn't protect her. That's my job. It's what I do. I pull people from car wrecks and buildings, but in my own home, I can't rescue her from a bad caseworker and a bad decision. And it just kills me."

I'm not sure, but I think there might be water in Dad's eyes. Mom's, too.

"I know it does. Sometimes I do feel like loving these kids and letting them go will kill me. Remember when Jade left? I thought we were all going to die of broken hearts. But we didn't."

"No, you're right. We didn't."

"Just think. If we'd quit fostering after Jade, there'd be six more foster kids who would have never been with us. Including Buddy. How could you say no to this little face?" Mom leans over and squeezes my cheeks. I smile real big and drool trickles past my bottom lip and onto her hand. She wipes it on Dad's sleeve and laughs.

"Nice!" he says and then kisses me on top of my head. "Did Stephanie tell you anything else about this Raphael?"

"Just that he was removed from both parents due to domestic violence and then was abused in his first foster home. He's only been in care for about four months. The plan is reunification with Mom."

"What did you tell Stephanie when she asked you if we'd take him?"

"I told her we were on hold, but I'd talk to you."

"Do you want to say yes?" Dad asks.

"Not if you don't. And that's okay. Really. Besides, things are so up in the air with Buddy's case. Maybe it's not a good time to bring another kid into the mix."

"Did Stephanie say anything else about Buddy's case?"

"Not much, just that overnights are inevitable. She did mention there's a court order about Raymond's girlfriend not being permitted to have contact with Buddy. I don't know why, though. It's a new girlfriend, not Buddy's mom."

"There's always something, huh?"

There *is* always Something Next. I know that for sure. I just never know what it will be.

Their voices drift off while my eyes get droopy.

I'm done for today.

CHAPTER 38

SOMETHING NEXT IS COMING AGAIN. I don't know what, but I can feel it. I don't think I like it.

Mom has been talking to me all morning about going to Raymond's house and sleeping there. I carefully watch every move she makes as she puts my things into a duffle bag.

"Come in!" Dad calls out when the doorbell rings. The front door opens and a man walks in.

"You don't look like Stephanie," Mom says to him.

"I hope not," he says, laughing. "I'm David."

The man holds his hand out. Mom shakes it. Then Dad does. I just look up at his long legs from where I'm standing. "Stephanie got stuck in court this morning, so I'm here in her place. She told me to tell you she's really sorry."

Dad reaches down for me.

"Buddy, this is David. Can you say hi?" I don't want to, so I just bury my head against Dad's chest.

"Hi, Buddy. Are you a shy little guy?" David asks. I don't answer. I wish I could pull my disappearing trick on him.

"Buddy, David here is going to take you to see Raymond at his house. X is going to go, too," Dad says.

"No go," I tell them. Nobody says anything.

"Do you have a car seat in your car?" Mom asks.

"I sure do. All set. Let's go, little guy." David holds his arms out for me and Dad tries to hand me over. They never used to let me go with people I don't know.

"I'll walk you out," Dad says, because I am still in his arms and don't want to leave, but I don't have a choice. The next thing I know,

I'm riding in a car with a man I've never seen before, and I don't know where I'm going or why. My heart is pounding so hard I can feel it in my toes.

Time for my disappearing trick. Maybe I can't pull it on anyone else, but I can pull it on me.

"Buddy, we're here. Wake up." I wait for a little bit before I open my eyes. When I do, David is lifting me out of my seat, but doesn't put me down.

It's a long walk past one building and then another. David stops, looks around, and then keeps going.

"This must be it," he says, but I don't know if he is talking to me. Maybe, because I'm the only one here. Or maybe he's talking to himself. Big people do that sometimes.

He rings a bell and there's a loud, crackly sound and then a voice.

"Hello?" I look all around because I don't know where the voice came from. There is nobody else but David and me.

"I'm looking for Raymond Morris. This Is David Lamping from Children's Services. I'm here with Buddy for his visit."

"Okay." The crackly noise finally stops.

I see Raymond and he pushes the door open for us.

"Nice to meet you," David says. Raymond just nods his head. I don't do anything except stay real still.

"So, which way are we going?" David asks as he shifts me in his arms.

"Up here. Third floor." Raymond points to the stairs. When we get to the top, Raymond leads us down a hallway and through another door.

"Buddy, you wanna get down?" David bends over and tries to stand me on the floor. I lift my feet so they don't touch. He pulls me back up and looks at my face. I look away, though, because I don't look in eyes.

"Does this mean you don't want to get down?" He tries again, and I do the same thing. "Raymond, why don't you take him?"

Raymond reaches out for me and David passes me off. Raymond's hands don't have sizzle, but that doesn't mean I want them.

David leaves, and it's just me and Raymond. I don't know what

I'm supposed to do now. I don't think Raymond knows what he's supposed to do either, so we both sit on the couch while Raymond opens my duffle bag. He pulls out X, so I reach my hands out for her and rub her ear between my finger and thumb. Then I hold her close to my face because she smells like home.

Raymond talks on his phone while I sit with X. Sometimes he gets up and I don't see him anymore, but I can hear him talking. There's noise at the door and I turn to look. Suddenly, it opens and someone walks in. It's a lady I've never seen before. My heart is pounding again.

"Raymond?" the lady calls out.

She walks toward me and bends down until her face is near mine. I don't know who she is or where she came from or what she wants, so I turn my face away from her and hold X a little tighter.

"Coming," I hear him call.

"So, this is him?" she asks as she straightens up.

"Yep, this is Michael," Raymond answers. I have no idea who Michael is.

"When's he leaving?"

"Tomorrow morning. Caseworker supposed to pick him up around eight."

"So I guess you want me outta here by then?"

"Yeah, since she said you ain't allowed to be here."

"Why you gonna let her tell you who you can and can't have in your own place?"

Raymond doesn't answer. He looks at her, then at me, and then back at her again.

"You got a light?" she asks.

"Yeah." He reaches into his pocket. "You can come back as soon as the worker's gone. She won't be here long. Ten minutes. Maybe less."

An old smell creeps into my nose. I don't like it, so I bury my face in X and try to make it go away, but it doesn't.

I wish I could go away.

"Let's go," Raymond says. It's the first time he's talked to me. He

177

never does that. I don't know how long I've been here, but it's not light outside anymore.

"Come on," he says as he grabs my arm and I stand. At least his hands don't have sizzle. "You don't need that thing." He takes X from my hand and throws her down on the couch. I don't know what to do, so I don't do anything. Finally, he picks me up and carries me out the door.

We head down the long hallway and outside into the dark.

"Put that boy down. He don't need to be carried," the lady says, so Raymond puts me on my feet. I'm happy to walk. It's one of my tricks, and no matter what, I take my tricks with me wherever I go, even if I go to places I don't like.

We walk a long way, and they are faster than me. I try to keep up, but my legs hurt and I'm tired. Finally, Raymond turns back and looks at me. He stops.

"Dominique, wait," he says until I get to him and he picks me up. Later, he opens the door to a place where the smells make my belly rumble. I squint my eyes because the lights are so bright.

"What do you think he wants to eat?" Raymond asks Dominique as he sets me down.

"Kids eat anything. Get him a hamburger."

"Can I take your order?"

I can't see who is talking. From where I stand, all I can see are legs everywhere.

"Yeah, gimme a combo number two and a Happy Meal with a hamburger."

"Do you want milk or a soft drink with the happy meal?"

"Don't matter. Soft drink, I guess."

"Is that all for you?"

"Dominique, what do you want?"

"Number four," she says.

We sit at a table. Actually, I kind of stand, because if I sit, I can't reach my food. Raymond holds a drink with a straw up to my mouth and I suck on it. My eyes get big and I cough a tiny bit. I don't know this taste, so I suck on the straw some more and cold stuff runs down my throat into my belly.

The hamburger looks so big that I don't know what to do with it, so I eat some French fries. Mostly, I just keep sucking on the straw and moving the arms of the plastic robot that came with my Happy Meal.

"Eat your hamburger," Raymond tells me, but I don't.

"Eat it!" Dominique squawks. She picks it up and tries to stuff it into my mouth. I choke and cough, but I don't cry. She puts it down. She's mad. I can tell.

"Maybe he's not hungry," Raymond says.

"He's wastin' food."

There's no more talking and no more eating, at least for me. I'm not hungry anyway and my belly hurts. I just stay real still.

When they are done eating, they put the hamburger back in a wrapper and stuff it in a bag. I climb down from the seat and we start walking some more. This time, Raymond holds my hand, and I'm glad. My legs hurt, my belly hurts, all of me hurts, and its dark and I don't like it. My belly feels worse and worse. I stop walking, but Raymond tugs on my hand. My belly rumbles, and suddenly stuff flies out of my mouth and nose, runs down my shirt and splatters on the ground. My throat is burning.

"Nasty," Dominique says.

"You got a rag or something?"

Dominique reaches into the bag and pulls out some napkins. Raymond wipes my mouth and tries to wipe my shirt, but the napkin crumbles into little pieces. He picks me up so I don't have to walk anymore. When we get to his place, he walks me to the kitchen sink and starts to take off my shirt.

"A little help here?" he asks Dominique.

"If I wanted to take care of kids, I'd have kept my own. And you don't see my kids, do you?" She's mad again. I make tiny breaths and wait to see what Raymond will do. I wait for the yelling and the sizzling hands, but they don't come.

He changes my clothes and sets me on the floor. I walk to the couch and climb up, because X is there and she is all I want. I climb back down and lay on the floor and rub X's ear between my finger and thumb and use my disappearing trick.

CHAPTER 39

I AM NOT AT HOME. I am not in my crib. I don't know where I am, but it is dark except for the colors that come from the TV. My belly aches and my bottom is all wet.

I stare at the ceiling and wait for Something Next. It never comes, so I pull myself up and the wet runs down my legs. I don't know what to do, so I stand with X for a long time and don't move. But since my superpower is not standing in strange places forever, I start to cry. Soft at first, then louder and louder and louder.

Raymond stands over me. His hands reach out. Still no sizzle.

He changes my diaper, but I don't think he knows what he is doing because it is taking *forever*. I stop crying and watch his face the whole time, because I know he won't look at my eyes. His eyes are too busy looking at the diaper he's trying to put on me.

He carries me into his bedroom and puts me in a play pen.

"Why does he have to be in here?" Dominique asks. "I told you to leave him out there."

"He woke up and was crying."

"That's what kids do. Then they go back to sleep. He don't need to be in here."

Raymond pauses. He looks at me sitting in the play pen then looks at Dominique on the bed.

"Make your choice. It's me or him, but we ain't both gonna sleep in here."

Raymond picks up the play pen with me and X in it and tries to squeeze it through the door, but it's too big.

"You're so dumb. That ain't gonna fit. Just leave it. He don't need it. He can sleep on the floor."

Raymond pauses again, looks down at me and X, and then picks me up and carries me into the next room. He lays me down, throws a blanket on top of me, and walks away.

I don't even have X. I curl up into a ball and wish my disappearing trick could work forever.

The next time I wake up, it is light outside. I feel around for X, but she isn't here. I sit up and look, too, but I don't see her. I stand up and wander around, pushing on doors to see what will happen. One door swings open and I see Raymond and Dominique sleeping.

I see X, too! She's in that play pen. The only thing I want is to rub her ear between my thumb and finger. I stand as tall as I can until I can reach the top. Then I lift one leg, then another, and I keep trying until my hand slips and I fall.

Climbing is not my superpower.

"What was that?" Dominique asks in a sleepy voice.

"Hmmm?"

"Where's the kid?"

Raymond sits up and looks around.

"Oh, he over there. What time is it?" he asks.

"About eight," she says. Raymond jumps out of bed.

"Damnit! The worker's gonna be here any minute!" He scoops me off the floor, rushes out the bedroom door, and lays me down on the couch.

"Where's his bag?" he calls out while his eyes run around the room.

"Look in the kitchen."

"You gotta get out of here!" Raymond yells while he fetches my bag. He comes back and strips off my clothes. He fumbles with my diaper, but he does it faster this time. "I told you, you gotta leave before the worker gets here!"

"I heard you the first time." She's mad. I can tell.

There's a knock on the door.

"Damnit damnit damnit!" Raymond says, but not very loudly. "You gotta hide."

"For real?"

"Damn right! *Now!*"

"Where the hell am I supposed to hide?"

Another knock. His eyes are running around again.

"Bathroom!"

Dominique disappears and Raymond opens the door. It's Stephanie!

"Good morning, Raymond," she says as she steps inside. I can't run fast, but I get to Stephanie as quick as I can.

"Good morning to you too, Buddy," she says. She stoops down so I can see her face. I dive into her, so she picks me up. "Looks like you guys just got up."

"Yeah. Tired I guess. I just finished changing him. Don't have his bag packed, but I'll hurry on and get it."

"Did he have breakfast yet?"

"No, I was just fixin' to get it when you came."

"Don't let me stop you. I'm sure he's hungry." She sits down on the couch with me in her lap. Raymond just looks at her and doesn't say anything before he walks to the kitchen.

"So, tell me all about your first overnight with this little guy," she says to Raymond when he returns with my sippy cup. I grab it and drink it down.

"Wow, that was fast! You must've been thirsty," Stephanie says and then turns back to him. "Anyway, about the visit …"

"It went fine."

"Did you have any visitors while he was here?"

"No, just us."

"No Dominique?"

"No," Raymond says after a pause. "But I still don't know she can't be here, too. We been together a long time."

"I understand you are a couple, but if you choose to stay with her, you can't have custody of Buddy. The court would never allow it, given her history of child endangering charges."

"It ain't fair of you all to make me choose between my girl and the boy."

"Well, it's not really about what's fair. It's about what is best for Buddy. And it's best for him not to be with adults who have endangered other kids in the past. The most important thing is for him to be safe."

"I'm just sayin' … she never did anything to him," he says.

"That's true, but she did abuse and neglect her own kids. Are you having second thoughts about wanting custody of Buddy? It kind of sounds like you are re-thinking things."

"No, I still want him."

"Even if it means you have to break it off with Dominique?"

"Yeah," he says. Stephanie looks at him long and hard. In the eyes. I've never looked in his eyes.

"Tell me about your visit. What did you guys do?" she asks.

"We didn't do a whole lot. We stayed here, watched TV, played some. We walked to McDonald's for dinner."

"I passed the McDonald's on the way here. How far is that? Half mile or so?"

"Somethin' like that."

"I wish I'd have thought to ask you if you had a stroller. I'm sure his foster mom would have sent one with him. How'd he do with going all that way?" she asks.

"He did good. He walked some. I carried him some. It worked out." Raymond hands me a cup of Cheerios.

"Was your visit harder or easier than you expected?" She pauses, and he doesn't say anything for a long time. "It's okay if you tell me it was hard. Toddlers aren't easy, especially if you're not used to it."

"It was easy. I'm glad he doesn't cry or scream or anything like that. He doesn't do much. That's good."

"I know that makes it easier for you, but it's really not good. His job as a toddler is to learn and grow and explore his surroundings. If he's not doing that, if he's just sitting quietly, then he's not learning and growing. That's a problem."

"Oh."

"Raymond, raising kids is hard. It's a twenty-four-hour-a-day job, seven days a week. It never ends. Even the best parents need support. It's a tough job to do alone."

"That's why I don't get why Dominique isn't allowed to be around."

"We've been through this. She doesn't have custody of her own kids because the court deemed her unfit to parent. She's done nothing to show she has changed."

I eat my Cheerios and wait for someone to say something. Finally, Stephanie does.

"Let's shift gears for a minute. Have you thought any more about calling Buddy's foster parents? They are open to that, and they know Buddy. I really wish you would get in touch with them. Most foster parents don't allow contact with family. You are lucky they do."

"I guess. Maybe I will."

"Why do I feel like you're just saying what you think I want to hear?"

"I don't know."

"Do you know any foster parents?" she asks.

"I did. Long time ago."

"Really? How'd you know them?"

"I was in foster homes for years when I was a kid, til I was eight. Then I got sent to live with my grandma."

"What was it like for you in foster care?"

"I don't remember how many homes I was in. None of them were good. One was really bad. Foster mom beat the crap out of me all the time, mostly for no reason."

"That's awful. I hate to hear things like that."

"I have a lot of memories of her. All bad. And the cockroaches. They were everywhere. Had to pick 'em out of my cereal."

"I hardly know what to say. You deserved so much better. For what it's worth, I'm so sorry."

"Ain't your fault," he says.

"Are you worried that's how Buddy's foster parents are?"

Raymond shrugs his shoulders.

"Raymond, I promise you, they are nothing like the foster parents you had when you were growing up. He is safe and happy there. I

know you probably won't trust me on that, but I wish you would …
or reach out to them and see for yourself."

"Maybe."

"Thanks for telling me about being in foster care. I'm sure it's not easy to talk about it."

"It's no big deal."

"I hope you'll think more about calling Buddy's foster parents. You can always just call to check in and ask how his day is going. Other than that, did you have any other questions?"

"No."

"Okay, then. Are you about finished with those, Buddy?" she asks as she stands. I guess this means I'm finished with them. She puts me down.

"Before I go, I need to see where Buddy slept last night."

"You already did that when you came out last month and asked all those questions. Why do you need to do that again?"

"Last month, you didn't have anywhere for Buddy to sleep. I need to make sure you got a playpen or crib since then. I would have checked yesterday if I had dropped him off."

Raymond walks toward the bedroom and opens the door. Stephanie steps inside and I trail behind her.

"Did you have any trouble getting him to sleep?"

"No. He slept right there in that playpen."

"Good. The playpen is fine for now, but you'll need to get a crib or toddler bed when he begins extended visits. I can get you a voucher for that."

"X!" I point to X. Stephanie reaches in and picks her up.

"Is this what you want?" I nod my head and she hands X to me. I tuck her under my arm and take the first deep breath I've had all day.

We walk out of the bedroom. Raymond grabs my bag and hands it to Stephanie.

"Thanks for showing me around. Just one more thing, though. Did you get child safety locks on the bathroom cabinet?"

"Yeah, I did."

"Great. I need to take a look before I leave." Before Raymond speaks and I move, Stephanie is headed toward the bathroom.

"Wait. I forgot, but I keep the door closed all the time anyway," he says, even though she's already opened the bathroom door and is standing inside.

"The thing is, as he settles in and gets more curious, he's going to be into everything. I had a case once where a little girl got into a bottle of bleach. Not good. We need to make sure we have anything with chemicals out of harm's way."

"I'll take care of it before the next visit."

Stephanie turns to leave the bathroom then stops suddenly.

"Do you have a cat or something?" she asks.

"No."

"Then why is the shower curtain moving?"

"It ain't movin'," he says.

"I'm almost sure I saw it move."

She pulls the curtain back and comes face-to-face with Dominique.

CHAPTER 40

NOBODY MOVES UNTIL STEPHANIE SPEAKS.

"I'm guessing you must be Dominique."

"You got no business telling Raymond who he can and can't have in his own place," Dominique says as she steps out of the bathroom.

"Raymond, you know this is against court orders," Stephanie says as she turns to Raymond.

"Those were all lies about my kids!" Dominique screams.

"We'll talk about this later. We're going to go now. Is this everything?" Stephanie pats my bag, which is on her shoulder.

"Yeah, it's all in there."

"Say good-bye, Buddy," she tells me as she picks me up, but I don't say anything.

"See you later, Little Man," Raymond says to me.

Something Next came this morning. Thank God it was Stephanie.

I climb out of my car seat with X after Stephanie undoes the straps. My feet hit the ground and I go as fast as I can up the driveway.

Mom is already out the front door and walking toward me. I throw my arms around her legs and then she picks me up and holds me tightly while she sways just a little bit. I don't ever want to leave her.

"Come in," she says to Stephanie as she opens the door and we all go inside. "How was his visit?"

"Well, it sounded like it went alright. But his girlfriend, who was ordered not to have contact, was there this morning. That's definitely a problem."

"I guess so."

"I need to talk to my supervisor and the GAL, but it's likely he won't have another visit. At least this week."

"You mean he might? Even though he violated a court order?"

"I don't think he should, but that's just my opinion. It's not up to me."

They keep talking, but I stop listening. I put my head on Mom's shoulder and rest in the safest place I've ever been. Here, nothing bad will happen. Finally, Stephanie leaves.

"Buddy, are you hungry?" I look up, but I don't say anything. "Stephanie said you had some Cheerios this morning and some milk, but not very much."

I climb into my booster seat and Mom fills a fresh sippy cup with milk. While I drink it, she cuts up a banana and puts it on a plate. I pick pieces up with both hands and stuff them in my mouth.

"One at a time," she says as she sits down at the table next to me. "Do you want some oatmeal, too?"

I nod.

"I didn't hear you. What did you say?"

"Yesh."

"Yes? Okay. Good boy." She feeds oatmeal to me until she says, "That's enough for now," even though I want more.

She wipes my face and my hands, which I hate *of course*, so I start to fuss. I used to always do that when she wiped my face, but I got used to it, so I stopped. Just not today.

"Let's get your diaper changed."

I stop fussing.

"You're pretty red down here. Did Raymond change your diaper?" I don't say anything. "Let's get you a bath. I hate to say it, but you're kind of stinky. Pee-eww!" She makes a funny face and scrunches her nose, but I don't feel like laughing.

She picks me up and carries me into the bathroom. I like to take a bath. There's things to play with in the bathtub that I can't play with anywhere else.

She starts the water and undresses me.

"Nice and warm," she tells me as the bathtub fills and she sticks her hand in it. "Want to get in?"

I nod my head and she holds my hand as I put one leg into the water and then the other and sit down.

She rubs shampoo on my head then pours water, but none gets in my eyes. It never does. I think it's one of her tricks. After a soapy washcloth runs all over my body, I play with my toys until suddenly my belly hurts. I stop playing.

"Buddy, you okay?"

I don't say anything because all that stuff in my belly comes flying out of my mouth and into the water.

"Buddy!" Mom scoops me out of the bathtub as fast as she can, wraps me in a towel and holds me over the toilet. "You poor thing. I'm so sorry."

More stuff falls from my mouth into the toilet below while Mom holds me and strokes my head. Finally, it stops, but not before I start crying. She cradles me in her arms and puts her hand to my forehead.

"Let's get you dressed and have a cuddle day. Want to?" I just keep crying. All my words are gone and I don't even know where they went.

Later, we sit in the big, comfy chair together. X is tucked under my arm and I lay with my head on Mom's chest. I can hear her *thump thump*. I love that sound more than anything, maybe even more than I love X. But X never makes me go away. I can take her wherever I go.

Mom covers us all with a soft blanket and my eyes get heavier and heavier until everything fades away.

The front door slams and my head pops up. I'm in my crib now, but I don't know how I got here. I reach for X and roll my head back and forth, back and forth and listen for the *swish swish*. I don't call out like I used to do. I just stay quiet and alone.

My door creaks open.

"Hi, Buddy!" Theo pulls me out of my crib. "We missed you!" I don't say anything. I just push on him until he puts me down and lets me walk by myself.

"Look who's awake! Somebody took quite the snooze today,"

Dad says. He walks toward me and I lift my arms for him but I still don't say anything. He picks me up and puts his hand on my forehead. "No fever."

"Maybe it was just a fluke. He threw up so much. We should go easy on dinner," Mom says.

"What's for dinner?" Theo asks as he opens both doors to the refrigerator.

"It's a Whatever Night. We have plenty of leftovers. There's lasagna and chicken chili. And lunchmeat, if you want a sandwich."

"Yes! I love those nights!" Theo says.

"Aren't you glad we work so hard on planning meals around here?" Mom asks Dad. He doesn't answer.

"Can we eat now? I'm starved." Theo is always hungry. "Can I make mac and cheese?"

"Sure," Dad says. "What about you, Buddy? Do you want some mac and cheese?"

I nod my head and climb into my booster seat at the table. Mom puts some crackers and a sippy cup of juice in front of me. I eat them all while Theo makes mac and cheese, and then I take a long drink.

"That went well," Dad says as he sits down with a bowl of steaming hot chicken chili. I love it. It's my favorite food. That, and cookies. I point to the bowl of chili while Mom puts some pieces of ham on my plate. I don't want ham.

"Eat your ham, Buddy," she says, but I don't want to. I point to the chili again.

"You want some?" Dad is blowing on a spoonful. I nod.

"That's not a good idea. I don't know if his stomach can handle it."

"You're probably right. Mac and cheese is almost ready. How about some of that?" I shake my head and start to cry.

"Sorry, Budster. What about this?" Dad asks. He puts some ham on my fork and holds it up to my mouth. I turn my head.

"Mac and cheese, coming up!" Theo puts a spoonful on my plate. I like mac and cheese. Just not right now, so I cry harder.

"Come here, Buddy." Dad leans over and picks me up, and suddenly there is sizzle everywhere—but it's not from his arms.

It's mine. It runs around inside me from my arms to my legs, back up to my belly and all the way to my head. It's so fast and so big, and I didn't even know I had sizzle! The sizzle makes me scream and scream and scream as loud as I can.

"I got him," Dad says as he carries me out of the kitchen. The sizzle makes my arms hit and legs kick as hard as I can, and I can't make it stop, even if I wanted to. Dad holds me tighter and keeps telling me it's alright and I'm alright, so I just scream louder, because he doesn't know what he's talking about.

It's not alright and I'm not alright. They made me go away. All of them. Dad and Mom and Theo and Iris and Esme. And now, all I have is sizzle.

Dad sets me down on the floor and I flop on my belly and bury my face in the carpet. As hard as I can, I pound my sizzle with my fists and kick it out of my legs. I pound and kick and scream until all of me is tired and my throat stings. Dad rubs his hand in circles on my back, but I don't want him touching me so I scoot away.

"How about an X?" I hear Theo's voice and then a thump on the ground next to me. I snatch X and stick her under my arm. I rub her ear between my finger and thumb and my screaming turns to crying. Dad moves closer.

"I'm sorry, Buddy. I know it's hard." He's rubbing his hand on my back again, and this time I let him. "Come here, Budster." He pulls me into his arms. He smooths the hair down on my sweaty head and hands me my sippy cup. I take a big, long drink.

"You're alright. It's all gonna be alright," he says again. My sizzle is gone, at least for now.

His hands never have sizzle. Not one single time. His arms are always safe.

Always.

CHAPTER 41

"We have no choice. We have to take him with us," Dad says. He's stressed. I can tell. So is Mom.

"Are you sure?" she asks him. "I feel kind of funny about that. I don't want to get in trouble for bringing a baby to the hearing."

I don't know who she is talking about, because I'm not a baby.

"It's juvenile court, for god's sake. It exists for the sake of kids, and if anyone has a problem with Buddy being there, then they've got bigger problems than they realize."

"I wish your mom wasn't sick. I'd much rather have him stay here with her," Mom says. "Are you sure one of us shouldn't stay home with him instead? Both of us don't need to go."

"If there's any issue, one of us can walk around with Buddy, away from everyone else. But we should both go. We're a team."

"Does that mean we should pull the kids out of school and bring them, too?" Mom smiles for the first time.

"I think we should draw the line on that."

"It was a joke," Mom says.

"Oh." Dad doesn't say anything else. I can feel the stress all over that one little sound.

"Uh-oh," I say, looking from one to the other. Dad starts to laugh for the first time. I love it when he laughs.

Dad pushes my stroller through big double doors and we wait in a line. I've never been here before. There are so many places to look, I don't know what to look at first.

"Cell phones, keys, anything metal go in the bin, bags on the belt," a man says to people standing in the line. He's wearing all black and has a hat on his head. The people walk past him, one by one, and sometimes there's a loud beep. When that happens, he tells them to step to the side and he waves a wand over them until he says, "You're good."

"Sir, put the bag on the belt and step over here, please."

"I got it," Mom says as she reaches under my stroller and pulls out my bag. The belt moves and my bag disappears. I have no idea where it went or if I will ever see it again. My mom walks through the box and it doesn't beep. Dad and I go around it to the man with the wand. He waves it all around me and my stroller and then all around Dad.

"You're good," he says again. He must say that a lot. Suddenly, my bag reappears. It's back! Must be one of the man's tricks.

We get on the elevator and a lady asks what floor.

"Six," Mom says. The lady pushes a button. It's very quiet in here, even though there are lots of faces. I look from one to the other, but they are all looking up or looking down. There is no smiling.

We get off the elevator and check in at a desk. No one looks happy here, either.

"Glad you could make it!" It's Stephanie. "How are you?"

"We're good," Mom says. "We feel kind of funny bringing Buddy to court with us. I hope it's okay. Will's mom was sick."

"It's fine. Short notice, anyway," Stephanie says. She bends down so her face is close to mine. "And how's Buddy today?" I don't look in her eyes and I don't say anything, even though I like that she always talks to me. Always.

"So, what exactly is the hearing about today?" Dad asks.

"Visitation with Raymond. My attorney filed a motion to suspend visits because Raymond violated the court's order and allowed Dominique to be there. Justin, the GAL, disagrees and thinks visits should continue as planned with the goal of reunification with Raymond."

"We've only met Justin once," Mom says.

"Looks like it's about to be twice." Stephanie eyes follow a man walking toward us.

"Mr. and Mrs. Jackson, good to see you again," he says with his hand out. Dad shakes it first, then Mom.

"And you are ...?" Dad asks.

"Justin Miller, Michael's GAL," he says. "We met at your house a while back." Who is this "Michael" person I keep hearing about?

"Oh, right. Been so long ago, I'd forgotten," Dad says.

"How have things been going?" Justin asks.

"Buddy's been having a harder time since visits with Raymond started, and he's backsliding a little."

"We expect kids like Michael to have a hard time adjusting to visits. It's just part of the process."

This man doesn't talk to me or even look at me. I don't like him.

"It looks like Raymond just signed in," Stephanie says. "I'm going to go talk with him. Do you mind if I bring him over to introduce you?"

"No, not at all. We want to meet him," Mom says. Stephanie walks away and Mom turns back to Justin.

"So, what do you think will happen today?" Dad asks.

"We're only set for an hour on Stephanie's motion to terminate Mr. Morris' visits. I doubt the magistrate can hear the case in an hour, and she's already running behind schedule. We'll probably just reschedule for a full hearing and testimony."

"Reschedule? How soon? Next week or ...?" Mom asks.

"Hardly. At least two months out. Maybe more."

"You're kidding. Why so long?"

"It's a typical wait time, usually longer. We have three attorneys on this case: mine, Stephanie's, and Raymond's—and all of their calendars are pretty full. Then you add the magistrate's schedule. By the time we find a common date that works for everyone, it could be weeks. Maybe months."

Mom and Dad don't say anything so Justin keeps talking. Maybe he doesn't like to be quiet.

"At least we don't have four attorneys anymore. Mom's withdrew after her client signed the permanent surrender. Since Mom is no longer a party to the case and doesn't have any rights, we won't need as much trial time. That should help."

"Excuse me," Stephanie says. Raymond is standing beside her.

"Mr. and Mrs. Jackson, I wanted to introduce you to Raymond Morris, Buddy's legal father. Raymond, these are Buddy's foster parents, Will and Maxine Jackson. And of course, you know Buddy."

I look up at the sound of my name. All these faces are staring down at me because I'm sitting in my stroller. I've never seen them all at the same time. It's a lot of faces.

"Hi Raymond, it's nice to meet you." Mom holds her hand out to him and he shakes it but doesn't say anything.

"Out!" I say as I lift my arms up. Dad reaches for me and pulls me onto his hip.

"Buddy, can you say hi to Raymond?"

"Hi, little man," Raymond says as his hand touches mine. I don't pull away, even though I think about it. I don't say anything, either.

"You know how he is … slow to warm up, always watching everything before he decides to say or do anything," Mom says. Raymond nods.

"Justin, can I talk to you for a moment?" Stephanie asks.

"Sure," he says and the two of them walk away. It's just me and Mom and Dad and Raymond.

"So, Raymond, we are really glad to finally meet you. I've been hoping you might call. I left a note with our phone numbers in the diaper bag, in case you wanted to get in touch."

"Yes, ma'am," he says. Mom and Dad seem to be waiting for him to say more, but Raymond doesn't talk a lot. He never talks to me. He's mostly quiet.

Justin and Stephanie reappear.

"The magistrate is still running behind, but since we are all together, let's use this time to talk about recent developments in Buddy's case. There's an empty room just down the hall. Why don't we move down that way?" Stephanie says.

Dad sets me down and holds my hand while we walk and Mom pushes the stroller. Raymond walks on my other side and slowly, his hand reaches out for mine, so I take it. Both of my hands are full now. I'm glad X is in the stroller, because if I was carrying her, I'd only have one hand.

When we get to the room, Stephanie and Justin pull chairs around the table and everyone takes a seat. I sit on Dad's lap.

"Do you want to sit on Raymond's lap, Buddy?" he asks. I shake my head.

"Are you sure? Look who's sitting on the table in front of him," Mom says.

It's X. I don't know how X got from my stroller to the table, but she did. And since Raymond's hands have never had sizzle and now he's holding X, I guess it's okay to sit with him. Dad holds my hand while I climb off his lap and over to Raymond's.

"Now that we all know each other, let's talk about what's going on," Stephanie says. "As you know, our current plan is to reunify Buddy with Raymond, which is why we started overnight visits after a series of day visits. His first overnight was not without concern. That's why we are here today."

Raymond sits very still, like I do when I use my disappearing trick.

"I don't believe one mistake should derail the plan or prevent reunification. The court prefers placement with parents whenever possible," Justin says.

"I believe we all prefer to do whatever is in Buddy's best interest. Raymond, Maxine, Will … I know you all care a lot about Buddy."

"How many day visits have you had with Michael?" Justin asks Raymond.

"I don't know. Seems like a lot." He looks at Stephanie.

"I want to say at least ten. Do you guys know?" She turns to Mom and Dad.

"There've been twelve total scheduled, but Raymond canceled three," Mom says.

"That's a decent track record. It demonstrates Raymond's commitment to Michael," Justin says. Who *is* this Michael person he keeps talking about?

"Man, why you keep calling him Michael when everybody calls him Buddy?" Raymond asks.

"Just because foster parents decide to rename children, that doesn't mean we should ignore their real name."

"I want to make something clear, Mr. Miller. He came into our home with that nickname. We didn't give it to him," Dad says.

"Oh. Well, foster parents do that all the time: try to make the kid their own, hoping reunification will fail and they'll be able to adopt. My apologies."

"Let me assure you my wife and I have had six other foster children, all reunited with parents or biological family. We also have three children of our own. So please do not assume we hope a foster child's parents will fail."

It is so quiet, I think they can hear my heart beat. I hold X while I sit on Raymond's lap. One of his hands is resting on my knee.

"Anyway, back to why we are here," Stephanie says. "Raymond, I'm concerned about you allowing Dominique access to Buddy. I don't feel comfortable continuing overnight visits when you completely violated the court order. We made it very clear to you that contact between her and Buddy is not permitted."

"That is a concern," Justin says. "Raymond, do you understand why Dominique cannot have contact with Michael?"

There's that word *Michael* again. It's quiet again.

My mom and dad look at each other. She is mad. I can tell. Dad's eyes are a little bit wide and stare hard into hers and he slightly shakes his head. He wants her to know something, but he isn't saying what.

"I guess. I mean, if you all say she can't be there, then she can't be there," Raymond says. "Won't let it happen again."

"Good. Okay, Stephanie, can we agree that Raymond deserves another chance at overnights with Michael?"

Before Stephanie can answer, words start flying out of Mom's mouth.

"I'm sorry, but we need to back up a minute," Mom says. Dad's face is white. She keeps talking.

"Mr. Miller, you keep referring to Buddy as Michael when my husband explained to you that he has been called Buddy for as long as anyone knows. In fact, no one even knows how or why or where he got his nickname. Maybe his biological mother gave it to him. It doesn't really matter."

She takes a deep breath. Dad is still white. I think he's holding his breath.

She's not done.

"When you refuse to acknowledge the only name he knows, you refuse to acknowledge him as anything more than a *case* you have to deal with. That offends me, and quite frankly, it's tragic. He is not a case file. He is not an item on your to-do list. He is a baby whose life is in the hands of the people at this table and this court. The least you could do is show a little respect for him. And for us."

"Mrs. Jackson, I'm sorry you feel that way. I did not intend to be disrespectful."

Nobody says anything. I haven't moved from Raymond's lap and he hasn't moved at all. I'm not sure, but I think Raymond's heart is beating fast. I can just tell.

"I'm going to go check on the magistrate and see if she's ready," Justin says as he scoots back in his chair and stands. Stephanie looks at her phone and then she stands, too.

"I need to find my attorney before he gets pulled into his next hearing," she says.

It's just me and Raymond and Mom and Dad.

"Urgh! He just made me so mad I couldn't keep quiet," she says as she turns to Dad.

"Well, at least you didn't cuss him out," he says.

"Yeah, about that. Sorry, Raymond. I've been known to drop an occasional four-letter word sometimes. What can I say?"

"Occasional?" Dad asks.

Raymond's arms relax. I can feel it.

"Stop it!" Mom says. "Don't make me sound worse than I am."

Nobody says anything for a while, so I rub X's ear between my thumb and finger and wait for Something Next.

Raymond moves to the edge of his seat and then stands.

"Can you take him?" he asks Mom. "I need to talk to Stephanie."

"Sure." She holds out her hands and I reach for them.

Raymond leaves.

"I wonder what that's about?" Dad says.

"I have no idea."

"The magistrate is still behind schedule. She's not ready for us yet," Stephanie says as she returns. Raymond walks behind her. Justin is behind them both.

Dad looks at his phone and shakes his head.

"It's been almost an hour. What a waste of time! Good thing you all aren't running a business. You'd be bankrupt by now."

"Why don't we all have a seat again?" Stephanie says. We sit, but this time I stay on Mom's lap.

"Raymond, I understand you and Stephanie had a talk in the hall," Justin says.

"Yes, sir. We did." Raymond sits, stiff as a board. He's not relaxed anymore.

Mom and Dad are looking at each other like they don't know what's going on.

"Stephanie told me you are no longer interested in getting custody of Buddy. Is that true?" Justin says.

"That's right," he says. His voice is so quiet I can barely hear him.

Mom and Dad look at each other, stunned. They don't move. They don't breathe. They just stare, but they don't use a disappearing trick. Something Next is happening. I know it is. It's so big, I can feel it everywhere.

"Can I ask what changed your mind?" Justin is looking right at Raymond, but Raymond still doesn't move. Finally, he looks over to Stephanie.

"Raymond shared with me that he doesn't think he's the best person to raise Buddy. Initially, he wanted to get Buddy out of the system. He was sure Buddy was being mistreated simply by being in foster care. But he sees that Buddy is safe and happy where he is, and that's all he wants."

"Are you sure?" Justin asks.

"I'm sure," Raymond replies quietly.

"Mr. and Mrs. Jackson, I'm sure this is news to you," Justin says.

"Yes. I hardly know what to say," Dad says. "We didn't see this coming."

"Can I ask, would you be interested in adopting him?" Mom and Dad look at each other.

"If Buddy needs a forever family, we'd love to be that family," Mom says. Her words are shaky and I can feel her *thump thump* get faster, just a little.

"Raymond," Justin says as he turns back to him. "You do realize that, if you sign away your parental rights and Buddy is available for adoption, that decision cannot be reversed. If, for some reason, the Jacksons don't adopt Buddy, you won't be considered an option at that point. The agency would place him with a different adoptive family."

"We're not going to change our mind, if that's what you mean," Dad says.

"Fine. I just want to make Raymond aware."

"I understand," Raymond says.

"And you're willing to sign a permanent surrender right now?"

"Yes. I'm ready."

"Justin, can you go find the attorneys and let them know?" Stephanie asks.

"Yes. I'll get the paperwork too," Justin says as he pushes his chair back from the table and stands.

The room is quiet again, but Something Next is still bouncing around.

"Raymond, I'm so shocked," Dad says. "I don't understand where this came from. I think I can speak for my wife, too, when I say that we are just blown away."

Raymond doesn't say anything. Mom reaches over and touches his trembling hand. It stops.

"Raymond, there has to be a reason you changed your mind. What is it?" Mom asks.

"Go ahead. You can tell them." Stephanie nods in his direction. He catches her eye and starts to speak.

"I was telling Stephanie that I was across town last week. Stopped at a Dairy Mart to pick up some cigarettes. I was in line when here comes Buddy, holding the hand of a little girl."

"That was Esme," Mom says quietly.

"You walked over to get some milk." Raymond paused. "And the little girl—Esme?—she and Buddy were looking at the candy. She was trying to talk him into getting' a Reese's Cup, but he kept saying no, M&Ms. And finally, she said okay and his face lit up like I've never seen it."

No one says anything. Happy and sad and all kinds of other things I don't even know are swirling all over the place at the same time. I can feel them inside me and all around me. I think everyone else feels them, too.

"I just want what is best for him," Raymond says.

"I know you do. I think we all want that," Stephanie says.

"I think your family is best for him," Raymond says as he raises his head and looks at Mom.

"I promise you, we will love him and protect him, no matter what. You have our word. We won't let him down. Or you," Mom says as they lock eyes.

"I believe you. I just saw you take up for him, sayin' he wasn't a case file and all that."

His hand reaches out for mine and I know he is looking at me, but I don't look in his eyes. I don't look in eyes unless they are eyes in my family, like Mom's or Dad's or Theo's or Iris' or Esme's. Maybe someday I will look in other eyes. Just not yet.

"You do good, Buddy," Raymond says as he turns to Stephanie. "You got those papers I need to sign?"

"Justin is getting them. Your attorney will walk you through everything. He's just down the hall. Let's go find him." She stands and they head toward the door. Raymond turns around one more time.

"Bye, Buddy," he says. Then he is gone.

"Buddy!" Mom whispers and holds me so close to her chest, I can hear her *thump thump* loudly now. I look up and Dad's eyes have water. My eyes swim in them. All of me feels right on the inside. I tuck X under my arm and hold her close.

"What just happened?" Dad asks. He's still stunned.

"Wow." Mom is still stunned, too. "I can only imagine what the kids are going to do when we tell them. They'll be ecstatic."

Something Next is coming and it's going to be alright.

I'm going to be alright.

ABOUT THE AUTHOR

HOLLY SCHLAACK HAS DEVOTED HER career to advocating for foster children. She is a former children's services caseworker and Guardian ad Litem charged with representing the best interests of abused and neglected infants and toddlers in court. She created and managed an award-winning program, Building Blocks, while supervising and mentoring Court Appointed Special Advocates (CASAs), and co-founded the Southwest Chapter of the Ohio Association for Infant Mental Health. She is a highly-regarded speaker who trains nationally on topics related to protecting and supporting very young children.

Holly is the author of *Invisible Kids: Marcus Fiesel's Legacy* and the founder of Invisible Kids Project, a non-profit dedicated to prioritizing the rights of kids in the child welfare system and engaging community to create positive change. As a voice of compassion, experience and common sense, Holly is routinely sought out by political and other leaders to advise on issues related to systemic and legislative change.

Holly and her husband, Ed, live in Cincinnati, Ohio. They are the proud parents of Hanna, Grace and Ben.

For more stories, tidbits and fun facts to know and share, please visit:
WWW.BOOKSBYHOLLY.COM

To request information about Holly Schlaack's availability for speaking engagements, please email:
ADMIN@BOOKSBYHOLLY.COM